TIME-STONE

Rescue
in the
MayanJungle

Written by
Karla Warkentin

Illustrated by
Ron Adair

Collect them all!

Rescue in the Mayan Jungle
Mystery in the Medieval Castle
Treachery in the Ancient Laboratory
Terror in Hawk's Village
Escape from the Volcano

COOK COMMUNICATIONS MINISTRIES
Colorado Springs, Colorado • Paris, Ontario
KINGSWAY COMMUNICATIONS LTD
Eastbourne, England

A Faith Building Guide can
be found on page 142.

Faith Kidz® is an imprint of Cook Communications Ministries
Colorado Springs, Colorado 80918
Cook Communications, Paris, Ontario
Kingsway Communications, Eastbourne, England

Rescue in the Mayan Jungle
© 2004 by Karla Marie Krahn-Warkentin

First printing, 2004
Printed in the United States of America

2 3 4 5 6 7 8 9 10 Printing/Year 10 09 08 07 06

Editor: Heather Gemmen
Cover Designer: Image Studios

Library of Congress Cataloging-in-Publication Data

Warkentin, Karla.
    Rescue in the Mayan jungle / written by Karla Warkentin ; illustrated
by Ron Adair.
        p. cm. -- (Time stone travelers)
Summary: The time stone transports Josh and his siblings into a Mayan
village where they try to save a priestess being held in virtual
slavery.
    ISBN 0-7814-4027-0 (pbk.)
    [1. Time travel--Fiction. 2. Brothers and sisters--Fiction. 3.
Mayas--Fiction. 4. Christian life--Fiction.] I. Adair, Ron, ill. II.
Title.
    PZ7.W2373Re 2004
    [Fic]--dc22
                                        2003020396

To Randy, with boundless love and gratitude

A big thank you to:

Elaine Wright Colvin, for guiding me through the process;
Mary McNeil, for championing the series;
Mark Sawatzky, for creatively pulling the concept together;
Dr. Gus Konkel, for help with the ancient Phoenician alphabet,
interpreting the Ten Commandments, and the encouragement;
Pastor Russ Toews, for the books and spiritual guidance;
Dr. Carl Duerksen, for willingly sharing your medical expertise;
my Westside prayer team: Wayne & Phyllis Banman, Rachel Dyck,
Ingrid Friesen, Linda Janzen, Cindy Klassen, Marie Peters, Mary
Poetker, Sharon Toews, and Grace Warkentin—words cannot
express how much I appreciate each one of you;
Erna Appelt, for sharing your books and prayers;
Chad Gemmen, for your many excellent suggestions;
and last, but certainly not least, my editor,
Heather Gemmen, who is truly amazing.

I am blessed to have each one of you in my life.

I would also like to thank Gary Dawson, missionary to the
Yanimami people, for the inspiration.

K.W.

I am the LORD your God,
who brought you out of Egypt,
out of the land of slavery.
You shall have no other gods before me.
Exodus 20:1–2

Visit the author's Web site at www.karlawarkentin.com

— ONE —

The Discovery

❈❈❈❈❈❈❈❈❈❈❈❈❈❈❈

Josh couldn't wait to get home. It was finally the weekend, and he didn't have any homework. Mom had promised to make barbecued chicken, mashed potatoes, Caesar salad, and her famous chocolate pie with whipped cream for dinner. And, best of all, he could tell his dad what the coach had said: "Josh may be the only eleven-year-old to make the team, but make no mistake: he's good. He's very good." Josh ran across his front yard, hollering out a challenge to his golden retriever.

Halfway to the house, he stumbled, almost tripping over a slight bump in the lawn. There, right below the grass, lay a perfectly round rock about the size of his fist, partially hidden by a thin layer of dirt. "Hey, Finnegan," he shouted to his dog, race forgotten. "Come over here. Look what I found!" Finnegan dashed across the yard to Josh but came to an abrupt halt just behind him and started barking.

"Finnie, it's okay. Come here." She barked again and growled as she backed away.

"You silly dog." Josh bent over and brushed the dirt off the rock's smooth surface. Suddenly, a small jolt of electricity surged through his hand and up his arm.

"Ouch!" he shouted, flapping his hand back and forth. "That

hurt." He looked around the yard but no one was in sight. "Where is everyone?" he mumbled, before marking the spot with his backpack and running into the house to find his brother. As he dashed through the kitchen, his mother looked up from the pie filling she was stirring on the stove.

"Hi, pumpkin. How was school today?" she asked.

"Where's Will?" he replied.

"I'll answer your question if you answer mine. How was school?"

"Fine. Where's Will?"

"Upstairs, studying."

"Thanks." Josh ran up the stairs and burst into the bedroom he shared with his brother. Even though they were twins, the two boys were opposite in nearly every way. Josh was blond, blue-eyed, and short—but surprisingly strong. Will had dark hair and squinty brown eyes that hid behind his glasses—and he was tall and gangly. Josh was outgoing and loved being with his friends; Will was happiest at times like this, lying on his stomach on his bed, his chin resting on the palm of his hand, reading from one of the books spread out across his mattress. Josh was smart, but pretended to be dumb, and never bothered to do his schoolwork. Will wasn't nearly as clever as he wanted everyone to think, but he worked hard and studied constantly—and always got good grades.

"Will, come outside. I found this thing! You've got to see it. It's amazing. It gave me a shock."

Will peered over the top of his glasses. "Can't you see I'm busy right now? Don't bug me when I'm studying."

"You have to come. It's important!"

"So is this. You're supposed to be studying for the science test, too, you know."

"I'll study later."

"That's what you always say. Did you tell Mom and Dad about your great big fifty-eight percent last week?"

"Fine. I'll get Ellen. She'll come with me. Study all you want. I don't need your help, anyway."

Will sat up, swung his legs over the side of the bed, and let out a big sigh. "Ellen's not home yet." He stood, tucked in his shirt, and ran his hands down the front of his pants to smooth out the wrinkles. "This better be important."

"Trust me, it is." Josh's long, blond bangs swished back and forth across his forehead as he motioned with his head towards the door. "Come on, let's go." He ran down the stairs and out of the house with Will trudging slowly behind.

"See, look," said Josh, pointing to the stone. "That's the thing I was telling you about."

"You dragged me out here to see a rock?" said Will, incredulously.

"Dig it out so we can take a closer look."

"I'm not touching it. You said it gave you a shock."

"Then what are we going to do—just leave it there? We need to take a closer look."

"You need some protection, something to break the current. Go get some gloves."

"I'll get some gardening gloves from the shed."

"No, I was thinking of something thicker. How about Mom's oven mitts?"

"Good idea. Aren't you glad you came out here? It's not every day you get to dig up something in your front yard wearing oven mitts."

"Look, you don't even know what this is yet. It'll probably turn out to be nothing, so relax, okay?"

Josh and Will had just finished digging a trench around the stone when Ellen walked up the driveway. She was fourteen years old, but often mistaken for someone younger because she was short for her age. Her brown eyes, like her braces, twinkled when she smiled. Her dad often compared her to their golden retriever—she was always happy and loved to be with people. Josh called her "mother" because she constantly bossed him and Will around.

"Oh no, here comes trouble," Josh grumbled.

"So what?" said Will.

"If she sees what we're doing, she'll wreck everything."

"Not everyone thinks she's so bad, you know. Riley told me that Jeremy likes her."

"Big deal. He obviously doesn't know her. He wouldn't say that if she was in his family."

Will laughed.

"What are you guys doing?" yelled Ellen.

"Nothing," said Josh. He looked at Will. "Maybe if we ignore her she'll go away," he whispered.

Ellen put her backpack on the front steps and walked over to them. "So much for that idea."

"What's going on?" she asked.

Josh looked at her over his shoulder. "I found this thing in the grass, but we can't get it out."

"Let me try." Ellen reached down.

"Be careful, it—"

She jerked her hand away. "Ouch! Why didn't you tell me I'd get a shock?"

"I tried to, but you barged right in, like usual."

Ellen glared at him, her eyes blazing, and strutted over to a near-by tree, her long hair floating in the breeze behind her. She grabbed a sturdy branch that was lying on the ground and marched back over to them. "Give me the oven mitts," she commanded. She put them on and poked the stick at the stone. The ground was hard so it took a few jabs to loosen it.

Ellen dug the stick in again. This time it touched the side of the stone. A small puff of smoke exploded out of it, and she jumped back. Finnegan bared her teeth and growled again.

"Wow! Did you see that? That was great," exclaimed Josh, grinning from ear to ear.

Ellen poked the stick under the stone again. This time it effortlessly popped out of the dirt. She flipped it to Josh with the stick. "I don't know why you're so excited. It's just a stone."

"We'll see about that," he replied.

"Just remember who dug it out for you. You wouldn't even be looking at it if it weren't for me."

"Right." Josh thrust his left hip out to one side and suspended his right arm in the air on the other, like the little teapot in the nursery rhyme. "Hi. I'm Super-Ellen," he said in a high-pitched voice, "and no one can do anything without me. I'm just so … so … so …" He paused, trying to find just the right word. "I'm just so wonderful, and you all need me so much."

"Mom! Josh is being rude again!" shouted Ellen.

When Josh's father arrived home from work, his entire family was huddled in the front yard. Josh's mother was standing in her slippers, apron, the white chef's hat she wore when she was cooking a big meal, and her oven mitts. She gently poked at the stone with Ellen's stick. Another puff of smoke burst out of it; she screamed and jumped back. Josh laughed, and Finnegan started to bark uncontrollably.

Josh's father got out of the car and started walking toward his family. "What's going on?" he shouted.

Josh ran over to him. "Dad, Dad, come look!" He grabbed his arm and pulled him across the lawn.

"What's Mom doing?" Dad asked.

"I found a strange stone when I was walking across the front yard after school. It has some weird writing on it. Can you help me read it?"

Josh's father put his arm around his wife. "Honey, what on earth are you doing out here in the middle of the lawn in your cooking gear?"

"Josh found something dangerous. The kids got a shock from it. If you touch it, it lets out a puff of smoke. We should call the fire department."

"Mom, it's no big deal. It's just a stone," said Ellen.

Josh's father bent down and picked it up. Another puff of smoke burst out of it. "Ouch," he said, dropping it to the ground. He waved his hand back and forth. "That hurt."

"See, I told you. That's no ordinary stone," said Josh.

Ellen rolled her eyes at him.

"Come on, you two, that's enough," said his mother. She turned to her husband. "What are we going to do about this? It's created quite a commotion."

His father slipped on the oven mitts and picked up the stone. "Hmm. Ellen, you're right, this looks like a stone—"

"See, told you," she said.

"—but I think it's more than that. These carvings are very unusual. I've never seen anything quite like this."

"What do you think they mean?" asked Josh.

"Let me see," said Will. He pushed his way past his brother. "Those markings are hieroglyphics, you know, like the ones on Egyptian tombs."

"Great. Now I've got Miss Bossy and Mr. Know-It-All," muttered Josh.

"Honey, dinner is ready," said his mother.

"We'd better go in and eat before Mom's dinner is ruined. We'll take the stone inside with us," said his father.

"Don't even think about bringing that into the house. It might be radioactive or something," his mother cautioned.

"But what if someone steals it?" asked Josh.

"I don't think it's radioactive, but we'll leave it in the garage for now, just in case. Let's go eat. We'll take a closer look at it later," said his father.

Ten minutes later, Josh shoved the last forkful of food into his mouth and pushed his chair away from the table. "Come on, Dad, let's go. By the way, do you think I could bring the stone to school?"

"Josh, you've barely finished eating. Don't you want dessert?" his mother asked.

"No, thanks. Come on, Dad, let's go."

"Mom went to a lot of trouble to make us this dinner. You shouldn't rush away," interjected Ellen.

"You know, my life would be a lot better if you didn't nag me all time," said Josh.

"That's enough fighting. Josh, we'll go out in a minute. We have to do our memory verse first," said his father.

"Can't we do it later?"

"No, we'll do it right now so we don't forget. Who wants to go first?" Ellen and Will put up their hands at the same time. "Okay, Ellen, you're first tonight."

"That's not fair. She went first yesterday," complained Will.

"Why are you fighting over whose going first on the stupid, oops, I mean, on the very nice Bible verse? It doesn't matter, we all have to say it," said Josh.

"You're right. You can go first," said his dad.

Josh frowned. "You want me to go first?"

"Is that a problem?"

"Only if he doesn't know it," said Will.

"Of course I know it."

"Whatever. This is going to be fun, watching you screw up."

Josh made a face at him. "'I know the plans I have for you,' declares the Lord. 'Plans to prosper you and not to harm you, plans to give you hope and a future.'"

"And ..." said his father.

"And what?"

"What about the rest? You're missing the second half."

"Um ... 'Then you will call upon me and come and pray to me, and I will listen to you.'" He whizzed through the last line at top speed. "'You will seek me and find me when you seek me with all your heart.'"

"I couldn't understand a word you just said. Next time slow down, okay? Who's next?"

"My turn," said Ellen. She recited the verse perfectly, as did Will.

"Thanks guys, that was great," said his father.

Josh stood up. "Now can we go outside?"

"Just a minute. What about your homework? And have you practiced your violin?" asked his mother.

"I haven't exactly had time, Mom. I've been busy ever since I got home."

"What about your studying? Don't you have a test on Monday?"

"Just a small one for science."

"Are you ready for it?"

Josh shrugged his shoulders. "Probably."

"Probably not," mocked Will.

"Mind your own business. Who asked you?"

"Nobody. Mom, you might want to ask Josh how he did on the math test last week, you know, the one I got ninety-eight percent on."

"Josh, is there something you want to tell us?" asked his dad.

"Maybe."

"What was your mark on the math test?"

Josh sunk into his seat. "Fifty-eight," he mumbled.

"Fifty-eight! You know that's not acceptable. That's barely a pass. What are you going to do about it?"

Josh flashed his father a hopeful smile. "Nothing?"

"We'll call Mrs. Andrews on Monday, and you'll have to re-learn the material at home."

Josh stood up and struck his teapot pose. "Study, study, study. Hi. My name's Will, and all I ever do is study. Study, study, study. I'm just so smart—oh, and I only get A+++s in school. Just call me Will, the smart boy."

"This is about you and your grades, not about your brother's. Now, go study," ordered his father.

Josh stalked off to his bedroom, and Will and Ellen went into the living room to practice their music.

A little while later, Josh slunk down the stairs and overheard his parents talking at the kitchen table.

"I just don't understand. He doesn't seem to care about his grades," said his father.

"I know. He'd rather be playing basketball. I can't say I blame him. Will said he made the team," said his mother.

"Good. I'm glad. There's nothing wrong with basketball, but he still needs to do better at school."

"I know." His mother sighed. "That son of yours is sure naughty sometimes. But you've got to admit, he does a bang-up imitation of his brother and sister."

"Why is he always *my* son when he gets into trouble? He gets his crazy sense of humor from your side of the family, probably from your father."

Josh sauntered into the room. "Just call me Gramps," he said, wiggling his bum back and forth as he walked towards the kitchen table.

"Were you listening to our private conversation?" asked his mom.

"I couldn't help it. I was just walking down the stairs, minding my own business, and I could hear you. It's not my fault."

"You need to be a little nicer to your brother. It's not fair to pick on him just because he does well at school."

"It's not just that. Look at the way he dresses. No one wears clothes like that to school."

"Josh, this isn't about your brother."

"You have different strengths," added his father.

"I know. You've told me that a million times before. I'm better at sports, and friendship, and being funny—"

"We all know what you're good at. Just because you don't like studying doesn't mean a fifty-eight is acceptable. We expect you to do your best."

"Okay. Sorry. Now can we go look at the stone?"

"All right."

His mother pushed her chair away from the table. "Just promise me you won't bring it into the house. It might not be safe. I don't want anyone getting hurt."

"If there's anything the least bit suspicious, we'll leave it in the garage for the night," said his father.

"Good. Have fun, you two."

TWO

A Strange Feeling

"Wake up," Josh whispered into his brother's ear.

"Let me sleep." Will rolled onto his back.

Josh tugged on his sleeve until Will finally opened his eyes again. "Sorry," said Josh, flashing his I'm-kind-of-sorry-but-I-really-meant-to-do-it smile. "Let's go to the garage and look at the stone."

Will lifted his head and looked at the clock. "Josh! It's midnight."

"I don't care what time it is. Let's go."

"Go ahead. You don't need me."

"I thought you'd want to come, you know, get a piece of the action," said Josh.

"You just don't want to go by yourself," said Will.

"Maybe."

"I'm not coming. I need to sleep."

"Come on," Josh whined. "It will only take a minute. I have a feeling about this, okay? Please come with me? Please, please, please, please, please?"

"We're not supposed to leave the house at night. What if we get caught?"

"We're not exactly leaving the house. The garage is part of the house, you know."

"Yeah, but—"

"Besides, Dad said it was okay."

"Are you sure?"

"Yes."

"All right, but don't ever wake me up in the middle of the night again. Promise?"

"Promise," said Josh, with his fingers crossed behind his back. He jumped off the top bunk and landed on the floor with a thud.

"Shh. You'll wake up Mom and Dad."

"Don't worry. They can't hear a thing over Dad's snoring."

Josh grabbed a flashlight from the top drawer of his night table, and the boys crept down the stairs together. Finnegan opened her eyes as they tiptoed through the dark kitchen. "It's okay, we'll be right back," he said, giving her a little scratch behind the ears.

Will slowly opened the garage door so it wouldn't creak. "Where is it?" He took one step down onto the cement floor and then quickly hopped back onto the mat on the stoop. "Hurry up. It's freezing out here. Where is it?"

"Over there, on Dad's workbench."

They moved stealthily along the side of the wooden workbench that ran the length of the garage. Their father's tools were arranged on a wooden pegboard on the back wall. Each tool had its shape traced around it with shiny silver paint. The metal of the saws and clamps reflected the little bit of moonlight coming through the side window.

Josh ran his fingers through the sawdust on the countertop. "There it is. Look! It's glowing."

"Don't touch it," ordered Will.

"What do you think I am, stupid? Wait—" Josh grinned. "Don't answer that. How do you think it got here?"

"Beats me. Maybe some freaky-looking aliens from another solar system were flying by, and they accidentally dropped it out of their spaceship window. No, on second thought I think they dropped it here on purpose so you could find it. Just think about it, Josh, you are so important that the aliens picked you for this special mission."

"Yeah, except the only freaky-looking alien I've ever seen around here is you," he replied, jabbing his brother with his pointy elbow.

Josh leaned over the workbench and aimed his flashlight at the stone. As he stood there examining it, it made a quiet whirring noise, and a small round hole opened up on its side. Suddenly the entire garage filled with light.

The boys took a quick step back. "What did you do?" snapped Will.

"I don't know. I aimed my flashlight at it and it started going crazy."

"Let's get Mom and Dad, quick!"

They dashed toward the door. As they entered the house, Josh looked over his shoulder. "Will, look!" he cried.

A jungle scene covered most of the wall beside their mom's minivan. There was a blurry spot in the middle of the picture that looked like a person running down an overgrown path. Then the light from the stone faded, and the picture on the wall disappeared.

"What's going on?" said Will, his voice trembling.

"I don't know."

The garage filled with light again. "Look, it's coming back. Go get Mom and Dad!"

They were at the bottom of the stairs in the front hall when

Ellen came out of the bathroom, half asleep. Josh skidded to a stop, but Will didn't see her until it was too late. He veered to one side, crashed headfirst into the wall, and then stood there, dazed, cradling his head in his hands.

"Ellen, come quick! Something is happening in the garage!" exclaimed Josh.

"What?" she mumbled in her sleepy I'm-not-used-to-talking-in-the-middle-of-the-night voice. "I thought we finished your French homework."

"This isn't about my homework. Something is happening in the garage."

"Okay, then I'm going to bed."

"She's sleepwalking again. You'll never wake her up. Let's get Mom and Dad," said Will.

"Come on, Ellen, wake up," Josh pleaded. "You have to come to the garage—now!"

"Not now. Maybe in the morning. Leave me alone." All of a sudden Ellen jerked her arm away and rubbed her eyes. "What's going on?"

Will let out a relieved sigh. "Good. She's awake."

"Something happened to the stone. It's going crazy," said Josh.

"What stone?" asked Ellen.

"The one I found on the front yard after school."

"Where is it?" They rushed back through the kitchen and onto the stoop outside the garage door.

"Oh, my," sputtered Ellen.

The garage wall was lit up with a picture of a big, gray castle. It was surrounded by a moat and a lush green forest that spread out as far as the eye could see. A girl peered out one of the upper windows. The scene faded, and it was replaced with a picture of a dimly lit laboratory. A murky black liquid bubbled away in a maze of old-fashioned glass tubes and beakers.

Ellen stared at her brothers, wide-eyed. "How did you do that?"

"That's the problem, we didn't." Josh swept his bangs out of his eyes. "The stone started doing this after I shone my flashlight on it."

The three of them stood there watching more pictures come and go. Will finally broke the silence. "We'd better get Mom and Dad."

Josh and Ellen ignored him. "Look, it's the jungle again," said Josh. A minute later the castle reappeared.

"There seems to be a pattern here," said Ellen. They counted ten different scenes, and then the jungle picture came back, followed by the rest once again.

Will pointed at the wall. "Look, now there's a knight at the castle." A knight dressed in a full suit of armor had joined the scene, and he was halfway across the drawbridge, on his way into the castle.

"There's the laboratory one again," said Ellen, "but look, it's changed too." A white-haired man wearing a long, flowing cape stood in the middle of the laboratory, scowling. A glass container lay on the floor, shattered, and there were tiny slivers of glass every-where.

Ellen walked over to the workbench. The boys trailed from a safe distance behind. "How do you think this works?"

Josh came up right behind her. "I don't know."

"Don't get too close. What if something bad happens? I'm going to get Mom and Dad," said Will.

"Don't wake them up. We don't need to bother them. Everything's okay," said Josh.

"Everything's okay? A stone with strange markings is project-ing pictures onto our garage wall, and you think everything's okay? I don't think so."

"What if we get in trouble for being out here?" asked Josh.

"You told me we were allowed out here."

"Josh?" questioned Ellen.

Josh looked at her, his mouth twitching.

"Do you have permission to be out here right now?"

"Dad said I could look at the stone some more. He didn't say anything about coming out here at night with you or Will, though."

Ellen groaned. "So we're not supposed to be here."

"Well, uh, no."

"If we get into trouble for this it's all your fault. I'm going to get Mom and Dad, even if it means you get caught," said Will.

"So much for your help." Josh spun around, and his hand accidentally brushed against the side of the stone. An incredible shiver traveled through his fingertips, all the way up his arm. He was so surprised, he grabbed onto his sister and brother.

Before he knew what was happening, the garage was spinning, the floor was shaking, and his mom's minivan was bouncing up and down like a basketball. Josh opened his mouth to scream, but nothing came out. A giant wave of sound crashed into him, followed by a blinding burst of light. Then everything went black, and a fierce wind pulled them down a long, dark tunnel.

— THREE —

The Jungle

What's that noise?" whispered Josh.

"I don't know. I'm too scared to look," said Will. He lay on the ground with his eyes scrunched shut. "You check."

Two yellow circles gleamed at Josh from high in the treetops. "It's an animal. I think it's a monkey." He slowly sat up and looked around. "Will, get up." His voice started to quiver. "We're not in the garage anymore."

A deep green canopy of leaves swayed in the breeze above them. Josh could hear the cries of tropical birds and the excited chatter of a group of monkeys—sounds unlike any he had ever heard before. The air was warm, and it smelled rich and thick like the wet soil in their garden after a summer rain.

Will opened one eye. "This can't be happening. It must be a bad dream. Help me wake up, please!" He opened his other eye. "No," he sobbed, as he saw the jungle spread out around him. "I want to go home."

"Where are we?" asked Josh.

"I don't know."

"Where's Ellen?"

"I don't know. Ellen … Ellen … ELLEN! WHERE ARE YOU?" The only reply was the high trill of a bird in a nearby tree. "This can't be happening. We can't have lost Ellen. This must be a bad, bad mistake."

Ellen moaned behind them. "Yes!" yelled Josh, pumping both fists into the air. "Thank you! She's alive! We're going to be okay!"

Ellen slowly sat up and peered over the bush-sized fern in front of her. She moved carefully, trying to keep her head as still as possible. "Where are we? I can't see very well. Everything's spinning."

"I think we're in a jungle, but I don't know why," said Josh.

"What happened? A minute ago we were standing in the garage, and now we're in the middle of a forest? This is too strange for words. And it's so hot," observed Ellen.

"Maybe it was time travel—you know, when people are teleported to another part of the world at another time. I've read about that," said Will.

"You've been watching too much television. There's no such thing as time travel," scoffed Josh.

"I've read about it, too. You can go to the past or the future. If that's what happened, I wonder which way we went?" said Ellen.

Josh stood up. "Shh! Be quiet. Did you hear that?" he whispered.

"What?" said Will.

"Over there."

Will turned to look in the direction Josh was pointing. "I don't hear anything."

"It's too late. You missed it."

"I heard some rustling. What was it?" asked Ellen.

"Someone ran by. Maybe it was the person from the picture on the wall." Josh pointed furiously at the overgrown path leading out of the clearing. "We're going to lose him. We'd better go!" He took two steps towards the path.

Ellen jumped to her feet, but was forced to grab a nearby tree so she wouldn't lose her balance. "What are you doing? We don't even know where we are. We need to talk about this before you go running off into the forest."

"That person was our clue, that's why he was on the wall. It's all starting to make sense. The stone made us time travel, and it transported us to the picture on the wall. Don't you get it?" sputtered Josh.

"I've never heard of time travel through pictures on a wall. Ellen's right: we need to think about this," said Will.

"No. We need to go before it's too late," said Josh.

"But what if we need to come back? We might need to be at this exact spot to go through the tunnel again."

"You're making that up."

"Am not. That's how it works in all the books I've read."

"What books?"

"You know, like the Narnia Chronicles. They had to find the wardrobe to get back."

"That doesn't mean this is the same."

"It might be. How are we supposed to know? I don't want to be trapped here forever." Will's eyes filled with tears. "I want to go home."

"I agree with Will. It's not always about you, Josh. You can't always have your way. We need to stay together and take things slow until we know what's going on," said Ellen.

"I never said this was about me. It's just that there's no point in standing here forever. We could be standing here for ten million years before someone comes along and finds us."

"We barely got here and you've already seen one person run by.

Can't you just wait a minute?"

"No. That person was our clue. I'm going now before we lose him for good." He walked down the path, picking up speed with each step as he left Ellen and Will behind.

Josh had traveled a short distance when he turned around and headed back. *I'd better not leave them*, he thought. *Ellen's probably having a fit by now, and Will can't survive without me.* He stopped when he heard their voices drifting towards him.

"What are we supposed to do? If we leave, we'll never find this spot again, and then we'll never get back home," complained Will.

"I know, but what if we lose Josh? If we don't catch up with him right away, we might never see him again either."

"That would be good."

"Don't be like that," chastised Ellen.

"We'd better follow him before it's too late. I can't believe he'd just take off on us like that."

"Well, I can. He doesn't care about anybody but himself. Let's leave something here to mark our spot. I'll hang up my housecoat. It's too hot to wear, anyhow."

If they're going to be like that, maybe I shouldn't wait for them after all. Josh watched as Ellen hung her housecoat on the highest tree branch she could reach so it was easily visible from anywhere in the clearing. Then she and Will started down the path towards him.

Josh quickly turned and jogged farther into the jungle, going fast enough so they'd think he'd been running the whole time, but slow enough so they could easily catch up. As he ran along, he muttered away. "I don't always think about myself. I help Will with stuff all the time. Ellen's the one with the problem. She's just mad because she didn't get her way."

Before long the three of them were back together, and they

continued on single file down the path. Giant leaves and long twisted vines slapped against their arms and faces. They ran as fast as they could, but no matter how hard they tried, they couldn't catch up to the person Josh had seen from the clearing.

"Guys," panted Will, "stop. I have to catch my breath."

"Do you have any idea where we're going?" asked Ellen.

"I can't see the person who ran by, but I'm sure if we stay on the path, we'll find him," said Josh.

"What if we're lost?" whimpered Will.

"I don't know where this path goes, but we're not lost," said Josh, with more confidence than he actually felt. "Come on, let's keep going." He jogged a few more steps before switching to a brisk walk. Ellen and Will trailed along after him.

The sun was starting to set, and it was getting darker by the minute. An owl hooted, its mournful cry echoing in the treetops above. The overgrown trees and bushes cast deep shadows across the path.

Josh stumbled and then turned around. "Look out for the … Oh, too late," he muttered. He walked back to Will and Ellen.

Will was lying face down in a deep puddle. Josh and Ellen tried to help him up, but he pushed them both away.

"Look at me," he exclaimed. He was covered from head to toe in slimy brown mud.

"We are," said Josh. He started to giggle.

"I'm soaking wet."

"You look terrible. Of all the people to get dirty, it would have to be you," said Ellen.

Will tried to wring the mud out of the bottom of his shirt, but it didn't work. It was so thick and gooey that it stuck to the flannel like glue. He pulled at the fabric covering his shoulders. "This feels horrible. What am I supposed to do?"

"Run around in your underwear?" suggested Josh.

Will scowled. "That's not funny."

"Guys, look." Ellen pointed at something a little ways down the path. "We're at the end."

Josh ran ahead and was the first one to reach the thick wall of rough, flat stones. Half a minute later, Will and Ellen joined him.

"Great. This is just great," muttered Will. "Now what?" There was nowhere to go and no sign of the person they had been chasing.

"I don't know about you, but I think it's too dark to go back. Let's see if we can scale this wall," said Ellen.

"Get serious," scoffed Will. He slapped a mosquito on his cheek. Two more quickly landed in its place. "Look at it. It's at least ten feet high; if you try to climb up the side, those stones will probably fall on you."

"Relax. I know exactly what I'm doing."

"Just because you took wall climbing at summer camp doesn't mean you're an expert. Besides, you don't have a harness or a helmet. If you fall, you'll crack your skull into a million little pieces, and I'm not interested in putting you back together again."

"I'll be okay. Think of this as a challenge. Josh, come help me."

Ellen bent down and Josh climbed onto her shoulders. "Up we go." She stood up, but when she tried to take a step, she stumbled. Josh grabbed her under the chin and squeezed. "Let go, you're choking me. Not so tight."

They stepped towards the wall, weaving back and forth. Josh rested his hands against the stones and was just about ready to stand up on her shoulders when he heard a muffled sound behind him.

Ellen turned. "No!" she screamed.

A crowd of fierce looking warriors armed with spears and bows surrounded Will. Two of them held flaming torches. The light from the torches reflected off the brightly striped war paint that covered their bodies, and their white eyes and teeth gleamed against their dark skin. One of the warriors held Will's neck in the crook of his arm, and he waved a long machete in front of his face. A wet drizzle ran down Will's legs.

In a deep, threatening voice the warrior holding Will said, "Ooma cum jumbo." He waved his machete again. Will turned pale white, his eyes rolled up, and his knees buckled. Two more warriors grabbed him as he slumped to the ground and propped him up by the elbows.

"Sheeya may lazlo!" shouted the head warrior.

"What's he saying?" whispered Ellen.

"He said: 'Where did you come from, and what are you doing here,'" Josh whispered back.

"You understand him?"

Josh nodded his head.

The warrior holding onto Will waved his machete again. Josh heard him say, "If you don't answer we'll take you to the Shaman! Beware of the Shaman!"

He and Ellen stood there, completely speechless. Finally Josh looked over to her.

"Do something!" she pleaded. Will was hanging from the arms of the two warriors, as limp as a rag doll.

Josh took a deep breath. One squeaky word came out of his mouth: "Canada."

"Ca-na-da? What is that? Ca-na-da? There is no such place. Ooma cum jumbo," he demanded.

"We come from a country called Canada. It's true. I'm not making it up. I don't know how we got here."

"You lie, child. Bind them," commanded the warrior.

Another warrior grabbed him, jerked his hands behind his back, and tied his wrists together with coarse, thickly braided rope. He watched them repeat the process with Ellen and then with Will, who had just come to.

Six warriors closed in around each of them. The head warrior strutted to the front of the line with one of his torchbearers, let out a loud yelp, and the procession started moving alongside the stone wall.

Josh kept trying to catch a glimpse of his sister and brother, but it was impossible for him to see past the warriors who blocked his view. They were big, strong men, and their muscles glistened with sweat. No matter how hard he tried not to touch them, he kept bumping into them, but it didn't seem to bother them as much as it bothered him.

Even though he was exhausted, Josh forced himself to keep going. When he slowed down to catch his breath, the warriors behind him stepped on the back of his heels. A little later, when he slowed down again, he felt something sharp press into his back. He turned around to see what it was. The warrior behind him gave him an evil grin and waved the tip of his spear between his shoulder blades. After that, every time he accidentally slowed down, he felt the prick of the spear and quickly picked up the pace.

Josh finally caught a glimpse of Will stumbling helplessly along in the twilight. One of the warriors beside him pulled out a machete. Will's eyes rolled back in his head, and the entire procession ground to a halt as he fainted again. The warriors guarding him grunted in disgust, grabbed him under the armpits, and the line started moving again, with Will's legs dragging in the mud behind them.

Josh spotted Will again a few minutes later. He had just regained consciousness, leaned over, and threw up all over one of the warrior's feet. The man leaped into a patch of tall grass and rubbed his feet back and forth, trying to clean them off. Another warrior grabbed Will and pulled him back into the line. He jerked his arm away and collapsed onto the ground where he lay wide-eyed and panting. One of the men picked him up by the waist and flung him over his shoulder.

"Don't hurt him. He's really sick," pleaded Ellen. The warrior grunted in response.

"Dear God," Josh prayed quietly, "please protect us. I don't want to die out here. Please rescue us and help us get back home."

— FOUR —

The Presence of Evil

T he procession stopped in front of an arched opening in the wall, about five meters wide and at least twenty meters tall. On either side of it were smaller doorways. Paintings of a sun, a jaguar, and several kinds of snakes covered the wall in brilliant shades of green, yellow, red, and blue.

Three warriors stood guard in front of the openings, each firmly holding a spear, ready to attack. The head warrior pushed Josh against the wall and jerked his arms above his head, pressing his hands into the rough stones. Will and Ellen were forced into the same position on either side of him.

"Shahkaya moonika," barked the warrior.

"That means don't move, and trust me, he means business," said Josh. He nodded to indicate that he understood, and the warrior nodded back before disappearing through one of the side doorways. The remaining warriors meandered around, talking amongst themselves.

"I feel like a criminal," complained Will.

"Oh, really? Imagine that. In case you didn't notice, we are prisoners," said Josh.

"Be nice. He's not feeling good," chastised Ellen.

Will bent over. His head sagged between his arms. "I feel horrible."

"Sorry. It's just that I thought it was kind of obvious we're in trouble," said Josh.

"Are you okay? Did they hurt you?" asked Ellen.

"I'm sort of okay." Will's eyes filled with tears. "Actually, I've never been this scared before in my entire life. Why are we here?" Tears dribbled down his cheeks, but he couldn't wipe them away.

"I don't know. Josh's stone had something to do with it," replied Ellen.

"Mom and Dad are going to panic when they wake up and find out we're gone. They'll probably think we were kidnapped," said Josh.

Will looked around. "I want to go home. I hate it here. Maybe if we touch the stone again it will take us back."

"But I don't have it. It's probably lying on Dad's workbench," said Josh.

"Then what are we supposed to do?"

Before anyone could answer, the head warrior reappeared. "Come. The Shaman will see you," he commanded.

"What did he say?" whispered Ellen.

"We're supposed to see the Shaman, whoever that is," said Josh.

"How come you can understand him, and I can't?"

"I don't know. Maybe because I'm smarter."

Ellen stuck out her tongue.

"I don't want to see the Shaman. Please let me stay here. I promise I won't cause any more problems. Please let me stay. Please?" pleaded Will.

The head warrior shook his head in disgust. "Come, NOW!" The guards formed a wide circle around them, and they slowly moved through the big opening in the wall.

"At least we're together," said Ellen.

Josh smirked. "Things are getting better by the minute."

They continued on silently, each lost in thought.

"Did you see those stone carvings on that building we just passed? There were some really creepy-looking faces," said Will.

"I think the wall marks the edge of a village. It looks pretty primitive," said Ellen.

"This whole place is spooky. It feels so weird. I wonder where we are," mumbled Josh.

As they walked through the village on a rough stone path, Josh saw little animals tied up in front of some of the stone buildings. There were goats, small black monkeys, and even a blue-headed parrot tethered to a tree, all of them peacefully sleeping. They didn't lift their heads or even open their eyes as the group passed by.

Bunches of palm trees were growing here and there, and flowered hibiscus bushes lined the sides of the buildings, partially shrouding their silvery white appearance. The only thing that broke up the lush green grass was the path. It turned every direction as it wound its way through the village.

As they rounded yet another corner, a magnificent stone temple appeared before them. It was four stories tall, and an imposing set of massive stone steps led up to a small square room on top. The stones were covered in carvings of snakes, skulls, mean-looking birds, and other strange animals that Josh didn't recognize.

"Wow," exclaimed Ellen. For the second time in her life, she was temporarily speechless. "We've definitely gone back in time. This must be an ancient village, maybe somewhere in South America."

"It could just as easily be Africa. They have jungles too, you know," argued Will.

"But the vegetation reminds me of South America."

"You guys have no idea what you're talking about. You've never been to South America or Africa. Quit trying to—ouch!" Josh crashed into the back of the warrior in front of him. The warrior turned and glared at him. "Oops, sorry," he said, rubbing his nose.

The warriors stopped at the base of the temple steps and formed a semicircle behind the kids. They stood completely still, with their machetes and spears tightly clasped in their hands, ready to attack if anyone made a wrong move.

Minutes passed by. Other than the palm leaves rustling in the breeze, the village was completely still. All Josh could hear was the warriors' deep breathing, in and out, in and out, over and over again, in a steady, unending rhythm.

Suddenly the warriors straightened up, lifted their spears, and struck them against the ground. Josh looked up and saw a man dressed in black slowly descend the temple staircase. His face was striped with thin red lines, and a long necklace of stained jaguar teeth encircled his neck. His bloodshot eyes peered out from under the hood of his cloak as he studied Josh and his siblings. As he walked down, he tapped each step with his long walking stick, which was topped with a carving of a snake.

"That must be the Shaman," whispered Josh.

A sinister smile crossed the man's face. "You are correct," he said in a deep, raspy voice. "I am Onamee, the Shaman of Quinaroo. And who are you?"

Josh looked at Will and Ellen, desperately hoping that one of them would answer, but neither of them said a word.

"I asked you a question. SPEAK, CHILD!"

"My name is Josh. This is Will and Ellen, my brother and sister."

"What tribe are you from?"

Josh looked at Ellen. "He wants to know what tribe we're from. What should I say?"

Ellen shrugged. "I don't know."

"We're not exactly from a tribe," said Josh.

"Do not lie to me. Everyone comes from a tribe. ANSWER MY QUESTION!"

"Okay, okay, sorry. We're from the tribe of MacKenzie."

"So, Josh of the MacKenzies, why are you here?"

"I don't know." He took a deep breath. "This might sound odd, but one minute we were standing in our garage, and I touched this stone, and then for some strange reason we ended up in your jungle."

"Ah, just as I thought. Your special powers from your God brought you here."

"Special powers? We don't have any special powers."

"Do not lie to me. Your powers brought you here because that is the only way people can get to our land. Our spirits sense your powers as well."

Josh furrowed his brow. "I don't know what you're talking about. I don't have any special powers, honest."

"You may not realize it, but you certainly possess them. The moment you entered our village, all of our spirits fled," he said, throwing back his arms. "They are waiting outside of the walls until you leave, and they want to know how long you will be staying."

"Well, I don't know," stammered Josh. "We, we … we didn't know this would happen. I don't know how long we'll be here."

"I told the spirits not long at all." A horrible laugh escaped from the Shaman's mouth, the sound of it so terrible that Josh lifted up his hands to cover his ears and shivered despite the heat.

"We're in the presence of evil. We need to get out of here," whispered Ellen.

"And I am in the presence of three children who worship 'the Great Spirit'—our enemy God," said the Shaman.

"Josh, did he just say what I think he said?"

"Did you understand him?"

"I think he said that we worshiped 'the Great Spirit,' their enemy. Is that right?" asked Ellen, her voice quaking.

Josh shuddered. "That's what he said."

"How come I can understand him now?"

"I don't know, but it's fine with me. You can do some of the talking. These questions are hard."

Ellen turned to the Shaman. "We don't worship an 'enemy God.' We worship the one true God who made the world."

Will grabbed her by the arm. "Ellen! What are you doing? You're going to make him mad. This guy is bad news. He might kill us."

"Don't worry, little boy. I have no plans to kill you, yet," said the Shaman.

Will looked at Ellen. "Do something."

"How do you know we worship the 'Great Spirit'? We haven't even talked to anyone here. I didn't tell your warriors that we're Christians," said Ellen.

"Young girl, I have great power. I can see into people's hearts, and when I look into yours, I can see your Great Spirit. He lives in you and fills your heart with light."

"You can see into my heart?"

"Of course. The Great Spirit who lives way up in the heaven beyond the heavens is inside of you. There is no darkness where he lives, and there are beings around him that continually sing. A crystal clear river flows through his land, and if you drink from it you will live forever." The Shaman grew more passionate as he continued on. "Your Great Spirit has fruit trees up in the heaven beyond the heavens, and if you eat of their fruit, you will never be sick."

Ellen stared at him, her mouth hanging open. "That's exactly what the Bible says about heaven. How did you know that?"

"My spirits have shown me where your Great Spirit lives from a long ways off. Your Great Spirit is the reason my people suffer. He sends sickness to our village, and he causes our children to die. Even though he has this wonderful, beautiful place to live and a river that gives life, my people are not welcome there. We fear your God because he punishes us."

"That's not true. The Bible says that God loves everyone."

The Shaman turned and began walking up the temple steps. He was halfway up when he stopped, turned, and stared defiantly at the group gathered below. "I will let you and your brothers live for now because I do not want to anger your God, but I suggest that you be very careful; if you threaten my people in any way, I will be forced to kill you."

"Don't worry. We won't make any trouble. I promise," said Josh, his hands fluttering in front of him.

"I trust that you will abide by the rules of my village. Guards, take them away." Onamee inserted his hand into the pouch hanging from his waist and waved his arm in a large circle above his head. A mysterious cloud of thick smoke appeared out of nowhere and completely enveloped him.

"Whoa! Did you see that?" exclaimed Josh.

"And he thinks we have magical powers. We can't do that," said Will.

The guards surrounded Josh, Ellen, and Will and led them off to a small hut at the side of the temple. Josh turned and looked over his shoulder. The smoke had drifted away, and the Shaman was gone. "I don't believe it. He really vanished," he mumbled to himself.

The guards shoved them inside the hut and pulled a curtain across the opening, plunging the room into complete darkness.

"Let me out of here. I'm afraid of the dark," wailed Will. Please … Guards … Somebody … Help!"

"Will, calm down. You'll be okay," said Josh.

"Come over here. You'll feel better if we stay close together," soothed Ellen.

"Where are you? I can't see anything," cried Will.

"I'm over here," replied Ellen.

Josh could hear Will scooting across the hut. "Ellen, is that you?" he whined.

"No, I'm over here," she called out from the other side.

"Oh, sorry, Josh. I didn't mean to bump into you. I can't see where I'm going."

"Um, Will, I'm sitting here with Ellen."

"Ahh!" Will screamed. "Help! There's someone in here!" Josh heard him scrambling across the hut towards them.

"Get off," grunted Ellen. "You're hurting me."

"There's someone in here. I saw his eyes. They're huge. He's going to get us!"

"I can't even see your eyes, and you're sitting on top of me. Calm down. You're overreacting."

"Ellen, I'm serious. There's someone in here with us."

"I gathered that. Hello? Who's in here? Hello? Hello?" she called.

Josh held his breath as they waited for a response, but the room remained silent.

"There could be someone crazy in here. What if he's planning to hurt us?" asked Will.

"He would have done it already, stupid," scoffed Josh.

"Quit fighting, you two," hissed Ellen. "Hello over there. My name is Ellen. Can you understand me? I want to talk to you." Some quiet sniffling came from the other side of the hut. "Are you hurt? Do you need help?"

A strange voice floated across the room. "Help. Help."

"What do you need help with?"

"Aawk! Need help. Need help."

"He doesn't sound very good," whispered Will.

"Why are you whispering? He can hear you, you know," said Josh.

Josh jumped when the strange voice broke through the darkness again. "Aawk! Hear you. Hear you." The words were followed by a loud screechy laugh.

"I don't think it's a he," whispered Ellen. "You sound terrible. Let me help you." She crawled around the hut until she reached the other person. "Are you hurt?"

There was only silence.

"Put out your hand. I've got something for you."

"What are you doing?" asked Josh.

"I'm giving her my bracelet."

"Why?"

"I'm trying to make friends. Give me a minute, okay?" Josh sat there, waiting patiently. "Here, you can have this. Now can we talk?"

"Okay," said a small voice.

"Aawk! Okay. Okay."

"Aqua, shh! Be quiet. I'm okay. They didn't hurt me."

"What's your name?"

"Luna."

"What a pretty name. Who's Aqua? Is she your little sister?"

Luna giggled. "Aqua is my pet bird. I named her Aqua because she's blue like the water."

"No way," exclaimed Josh. "I have a goldfish named Mrs. Simpson. I named her after my old piano teacher because I was so happy when my mom finally let me quit taking lessons."

"That was my brother, Josh. My other brother Will is here, too. He's the one who bumped into you. Come over here, guys. We're here because we got into trouble with the Shaman."

"Did you see him disappear in that cloud of smoke? I wonder how he did it," said Josh.

"The Shaman knows magic. He can disappear and reappear again, and sometimes he even turns into a jaguar," noted Luna.

"A jaguar? No way!"

"He's a very powerful man. Be careful around him."

"Thanks for the warning. Why are you here?" asked Ellen.

"Sharjay, a Shaman from the neighboring village, came here today. He said that I caused the death of one of the girls in his village, but it's not true! I've never even met the girl who died."

"If you never met the girl, how can they blame you? That doesn't make sense," remarked Will.

"That's just how it is."

"We must be missing something. This Sharjay guy came to your village, blamed you for someone's death, and then you got thrown in here? His word was enough to make them lock you up, just like that?" asked Ellen.

"When someone dies, someone else always has to get blamed. I guess it was my turn."

"But what if someone gets sick and dies? Or what if they have an accident and get killed? It's not always someone's fault. Sometimes bad things just happen. Kind of like us coming here," Will added.

"It doesn't matter. When someone dies, their family goes to the Shaman, and they ask him whose fault it was. He usually tells them it was someone from another village."

"So why did he pick you?" asked Josh.

"Because he's mad at my father. My father was a great warrior, and he saved our village when Sharjay's tribe attacked."

"Now you're making sense. This Sharjay guy picked you so he could get revenge," declared Will.

"So what happens now?" asked Ellen.

"Sharjay will probably send one of his people to kill someone from my village. The only good thing about being trapped in here is that if that happens, it won't be me because the guards will protect me."

Just then the guards pulled the curtain open so they could check on their prisoners. A shaft of moonlight flooded the inside of the hut with light, and Luna spotted Ellen and the twins sitting cross-legged on the floor in front of her. She gasped, and her hand flew over her mouth. "What's wrong with you? Are you sick?"

"No. Why would you say that?" asked Ellen.

"Your skin—it's so white. There must be something wrong with you. I've never seen anyone like that before."

"Almost everybody looks like this where we come from," said Josh.

"Everyone in my village is going to stare at you. They might laugh, too."

"Thanks for the warning. Does it bother you?"

"Sort of. I might get into more trouble if anyone sees me with you."

"Great," muttered Will. "Just great."

"We'd better get some rest. We can worry about this in the morning. Hopefully they'll let us go," said Ellen.

"But I don't want to go to sleep," protested Josh.

"Who knows what tomorrow will bring. We need to be ready for anything. The more rest we get, the better."

"Okay," grumbled Josh.

Luna fell asleep with Aqua perched on her shoulder, the bird's head tucked under its wing. Josh couldn't get comfortable on the hard-packed dirt floor. He huddled close to Ellen and Will and tried to stay warm. Every few minutes a mosquito buzzed by his head, and he halfheartedly slapped at it. The excitement of the day finally gave way to weariness, and he drifted off into a restless sleep.

High in the temple above, the Shaman stood outside of the upper rooms and looked down on the hut where the kids were sleeping. He stroked his chin with his hand and deliberately forced his muscles to relax as he entered a trance-like state, softly chanting the words, "Hoya may cukumba," under his breath. When he was finished, he raised his hands high above his head, clenched his fists, and repeated the words once again.

From out of nowhere, a cloud drifted across the sky and blocked the light from the full moon. A sinister smile crossed Onamee's face. "Cha is in my favor again. I will triumph, and our visitors will be eliminated."

FIVE

Breaking the Rules

The sun was barely up when the curtains to the hut were ripped open. "Luna, your brother is here," announced one of the burly guards.

A tall, lean teenage boy entered the hut. His dark hair was cropped close to his head, and he smiled, showing off a row of beautiful white teeth. Luna squealed with delight and ran into his arms. "You found me!"

Aqua flew over to them and landed on Luna's shoulder. "Aawk. Me. Me," she squawked.

"You silly bird," said Puma. "Luna, why are you in here? You never get in trouble. What happened?"

Luna burst into tears. "A young girl died in Sharjay's village, and I got blamed. You and Mother were out picking fruit when they came to get me. I don't even know the girl who died. It wasn't my fault, honest. I didn't have anything to do with it."

"I know, I know. Sharjay is still trying to get revenge. You'd think he'd have given up by now, the old fool. Don't worry. It doesn't matter. I just spoke with Onamee, and he said he'd release you. He's making an exception for you because of our status in the village."

"He said I could go?" gasped Luna.

"Yes, he said you could go." Puma gave her another smile.

"Oh, Puma. Thank you!"

"Aawk. Thank you. Thank you."

Puma stroked the bird's feathered head. "You're something else, you crazy bird." He turned to Luna. "Cha is smiling down on us this morning. It's a good day."

"No, it's a great day!" she shouted, and she hugged him again. "Oh, I forgot to introduce you to my new friends." She pointed at Josh, Will, and Ellen, who were standing in the shadows behind them.

Puma stared at them, wide-eyed, before stepping back and holding out his hands. "Get away, spirits. Leave this village. You're not welcome here."

"Stop it. They aren't spirits—they're real just like you and me. You don't need to be afraid," said Luna.

"Fear is not the problem. Who are you? What are you doing in our village?"

"Puma, be nice," insisted Luna.

"It's okay. It must be a shock seeing people with white skin. No wonder you thought we were ghosts," said Ellen.

Puma eyed her suspiciously. "Now I know why Onamee said there was someone in the hut I needed to stay with. There's no way you'd survive in our village without protection. Your lives are in danger here."

"We have to stay with you?" groaned Will. "I thought we were going home."

"Onamee said he'd release the three of you and Luna as long as we stay together. You won't have any trouble if you're with me."

"But what if we don't want to go with you?"

"Will! If we stay with him, they'll let us out of here. Isn't that what you want?" asked Ellen.

"I suppose, but what if I don't want to go with him?"

"I'm not happy about this either. I've got better things to do than to watch out for three funny-looking strangers, especially a grubby one like you," said Puma, pointing to Will, "but those are the rules."

"See? That's why I don't want to be with him. It's obvious he doesn't want to be with me," moaned Will.

"I don't think we have a choice. Let's try to make the best of it, okay?" pleaded Ellen.

"You can count me in. I could use a change of scenery," said Josh.

"So what are your names?" asked Puma as they walked through the village together.

"I'm Ellen, and these are my brothers, Josh and Will."

"You're the first person I've ever met with the name Puma," said Will.

"It's a very good name," added Josh.

"When I was born, my father chose this name for me because he hoped I would be strong, quick, and fierce like the pumas who live in the jungle."

"Pumas? You're telling me that there are killer pumas in the jungle we ran through last night?" sputtered Ellen.

"We don't worry about them too much. If you make lots of noise while you walk, you'll probably be okay. It's the anacondas, scorpions, and tarantulas you have to worry about. Anacondas hunt in standing water and at the edge of the river; so if you stay away from those kinds of places, you'll be fine. Scorpions and tarantulas aren't life threatening, but they can sure sting."

"Oh, great," said Ellen, her face as white as a sheet.

"What's an anaconda?" asked Josh.

"A very large snake that squeezes its prey to death. Trust me, you don't want to meet one."

"I was just about to ask you if you'd take us to the clearing we landed in, but now I'm not so sure. I was hoping we might find a clue there that would help us get home," said Ellen.

"The police are probably searching for us right now. Mom and Dad must be terribly worried," declared Will.

"I bet Mom's sitting in her rocking chair, crying her eyes out," added Josh.

Puma stopped in front of a large stone building, the home of the market. A crowd of people surrounded the merchant's stalls, bargaining loudly for pieces of cloth, ground maize, and metal tools. There were groups of children everywhere. Some played tag and others crouched in the dirt, absorbed in a game that used little rocks.

Puma pointed to a small white stone building beside the market. "That's the home of the village healer. We go see her when we're sick, and she makes special teas and soups for us."

"They taste pretty bad, but they usually make you feel better," said Luna.

As they walked through the village, people stuck their heads out of their windows and doors and stared at Josh and his brother and sister. A mother walking towards them grabbed her small child and ran into the nearest building. Some of the villagers pointed and laughed.

"Look, there's a lady getting water," said Josh. A young woman was leaning over the village well, pulling up a bucket of water with a rope. Once her bucket was out, she set it down on the ground beside her, coiled the long rope, and placed it on top of her head with the end dangling down her back.

Josh walked over to get a closer look. When she spotted him, she backed away. "Get away, evil spirit! Be gone!" she shouted.

"I'm not an evil spirit. I just want to see your well."

"Be gone. Leave this village!"

Puma walked over and put his hand on her shoulder. They talked so fast that Josh couldn't understand most of what they were saying, but he did manage to catch a few phrases. "He's not an evil spirit … No, he's with me … Yes, Onamee knows he's here."

The woman gave Puma a look of disbelief, and bent down to pick up her bucket of water. It accidentally tipped and spilled across the path. She became so flustered that the rope fell off her head, and forgetting about the water, she picked up her empty bucket and backed down the path.

Josh grabbed one end of her rope. "Wait, you forgot this."

She flapped her arms at him. "Be gone, be gone!" she shouted.

Josh dropped the rope in the middle of the path and walked back to the group. "I feel like such a freak. This is embarrassing."

"Did you honestly think no one would notice your pale skin and funny clothes?" asked Puma.

"You're right; I suppose they would, but I didn't know I'd feel like such a loser."

"Aawk. Loser. Loser," squawked Aqua.

Puma led them to a bunch of simple round huts. They were lined up in tidy rows and ran from the house of the healer to the stone wall that marked the edge of the village. Thick wooden pillars supported the straw-covered roofs. Their sides had been left open so the breeze could drift through. Inside the huts, hammocks hung from the posts, and baskets and a variety of nets were arranged neatly on the dirt floors.

"Who lives there?" asked Josh.

"Those are the homes for the field workers. They live in the village between the planting and harvesting of the crops. We grow maize, plantains, sugar cane, and harvest mangos, too," explained Puma.

"And don't forget the avocadoes," added Luna.

Puma led them back to the center of the village. A two-toed sloth slowly crossed the path in front of them, and spider monkeys swung wildly through the treetops at breakneck speeds.

Ellen had to duck when a tiny baby monkey came flying through the air and crashed into a tree in front of her. She ran over to it. "Oh, you poor thing," she said, cradling it in her hands. "You'd better be more careful. You could really get hurt."

"Just leave it. It will be all right," said Puma.

"Are you sure? I'd hate to leave the little guy all alone."

Puma pointed to a tall palm tree behind her. "His mother is sitting in that tree, waiting for you to get out of the way so she can take over."

Ellen looked up. The mother monkey glared angrily at her.

She gave the baby monkey one last pat. "Okay, I get the hint."

"How many people live in your village?" asked Will.

"About two hundred," replied Luna.

"Do you go to school?"

"School?"

"I guess that answers my question."

"What do you do for fun?" asked Josh.

"I like to watch the ball game. They play it every other night."

"No way! Is it baseball or basketball?"

Luna gave him a blank look. "I don't know."

"Maybe you can show it to me later. How often do you eat?"

"Usually two or three times a day. Today we missed the morning meal, though, since Puma had to come get me."

"Really?" He gave Luna his best sad-puppy-dog face. "I'm starving."

Finally they arrived back at the temple. "Here we are, back where we started yesterday. Your Shaman is one scary guy," declared Josh.

"I suppose you might think that if you don't know him, but I think he's more wise than anything," said Puma.

"I don't know about the wise part. All I know is that he scares me."

"I bet you'll change your mind once you get to know him."

"Get to know him? You've got to be kidding. That's the last thing I want to do. As far as I'm concerned, the less we have to do with him, the better," said Will.

"Where does he live?" asked Josh.

"See that opening up there?" Puma pointed to the little building on top of the temple. "It leads to the sacred room where the altar is kept. The Shaman lives behind there."

"Yesterday I saw him disappear in a cloud of smoke, and Luna said he can turn into a jaguar. How does he do that?"

Puma looked around to ensure they were alone before he answered. "It's the power of his magic," he whispered.

"Magic?" stammered Will.

"That's why he's the most powerful man in the village. He can make life very difficult for people he doesn't like."

Will gave Puma a worried look. "Are you saying he doesn't like us?" He crossed his arms tightly against his chest and held his breath as he waited for Puma's reply.

"I'm not sure. He let you go—that really surprised me—and he told me to keep track of you. That's a good thing. He's never done that before. It's just that he usually goes to great lengths to keep strangers out of our village. For some reason, he's decided to make an exception for you. If I were you, I'd be careful."

"Aawk. Be careful. Be careful," said Aqua.

"All right, all right. I get the hint," grumbled Will.

"Aawk. Get hint. Get hint."

"Stupid bird," muttered Will under his breath. "So Puma, what's the story behind those carvings on the temple?"

"Isn't it funny how Will tries to change the subject whenever he's embarrassed?" observed Josh.

"It usually works," said Ellen. She smiled.

"Those carvings, they look pretty scary," remarked Will.

"He's trying to ignore us," said Josh.

Will gave his brother a dirty look. "Luna, why do you have a carving of a snake on top of your temple?"

"That's our serpent, Cha," she replied in a solemn voice.

"Oh, so that's Cha. Now I know who you were talking about before. I didn't want to look stupid, so I didn't ask," said Josh.

Puma shook his head. "That could be a fatal mistake in our village. If there's something you're not sure about, ask Luna or me. I'd hate to see you get into trouble just because you were too embarrassed to ask us about something.

"Each one of those skulls on the staircase represents a man from our village who died honorably in battle. The next village over is much poorer. They pick fights with us from time to time. It gives them an excuse to try to steal our tools and supplies."

"Is that the village that accused Luna of the girl's death?" asked Will.

"You have a good memory," observed Puma.

Will beamed.

"Sharjay, their Shaman, still makes trouble for us. He can't get past the walls anymore, though. Cha protects us from them." Puma planted his feet firmly on the ground and raised his right hand into the air. "Cha is the strongest and mightiest of the gods!" he shouted as he pumped his fist up and down.

A chill ran up Josh's spine. "Oh, boy. I can see we're going to have trouble with this Cha thing."

Ellen walked over to the edge of the temple. Just as she was about to step onto the bottom stair, Puma grabbed her from behind and shoved her to the ground.

"What are you doing?" he asked, his teeth clenched and eyes blazing. "You can't touch the sacred temple. You're not worthy! If the guards see you, it's over."

"What? I didn't do anything."

"Yes, you did! You were going to step on the sacred temple!"

"But … but … but I didn't."

Six guards came out from behind the temple. Before anyone realized what was happening, one of them grabbed Ellen by the arm and pulled her to her feet, and the rest of them surrounded her.

As she was being led away, she turned to her brothers. Tears filled her eyes. "Sorry," she cried.

"Aawk. Sorry. Sorry," said Aqua.

"Great. Now what?" groaned Will.

— SIX —

Underwater Attack

Josh stood next to the temple with Will, Puma, and Luna. He had no idea what to do, but was saved from making a decision when the Shaman descended the stairs. "What seems to be the problem, Puma?" he asked.

"That girl, Ellen, was about to set foot on the temple. I stopped her just in time from breaking the ancient tradition."

"No one told us anything about an ancient tradition," added Josh.

"Your sister was unaware of the rules?" asked the Shaman.

"There's no way Ellen would have deliberately done anything wrong. She's not like that. It's hard for us to do the right thing when we don't even know what it is."

"Puma, perhaps you have been a bit harsh with the girl. I know you are trying to do things correctly, but sometimes we can make exceptions and show mercy."

"But, Onamee," protested Puma.

"This is not your decision. It is mine. Boys, consider yourselves warned. If you or your sister break the ancient tradition again, you will be severely punished. Do you understand?"

They nodded.

"Good. I will instruct the guards to release her." He strode off towards the hut.

A minute later Ellen came running back. She wrapped her arms around her brothers. "I thought they were going to kill me. I'm so glad I'm still alive and that we're all together again."

"Ellen, get a grip. You were only gone for five minutes," said Josh. He pried her arms off his shoulders. "Everything's okay."

"I thought I'd never see you again," she said, sniffling as she gave him another hug.

Josh rolled his eyes. "Okay, okay, I get the picture. Let go. You're embarrassing me."

"Sorry. I can't help it." She wiped her tears with her sleeve. "Let's stay together, okay, no matter what."

"It's a deal, if you promise not to hug me in public," said Josh.

She smiled. "Okay, I'll try not to." Ellen turned to Puma. "I need to apologize. I'm sorry. I didn't mean to offend you. I've never been here before, and I didn't know I couldn't step there." There was a long pause as they stared at each other. "Will you please forgive me?"

A look of relief washed over his face. "Of course. How could you have known? I'm sorry I pushed you. I shouldn't have done that. It's just that I don't ever want to do anything to offend Cha. Cha is the strongest and the mightiest of the gods!" he shouted, pumping his fist into the air.

Josh looked at his brother and twirled his index finger in a circle by the side of his head before pointing to Puma.

Will gave him a dirty look. "Don't make more trouble."

"You've got to admit, he's a little cuckoo," whispered Josh.

"Luna, let's take everyone home for some lunch," said Puma.

Josh grinned. "On second thought, he's just fine."

As they walked through the village, a little girl ran up to Josh. "Hi," she said, shyly. He knelt down so they were at eye level, and she reached up and touched his blond hair. "Oooh."

Will smiled. "She likes you."

"How old are you?" asked Josh.

The little girl stared at him with her big brown eyes, not saying a word. "Hmm. Maybe you don't know about birthdays here."

The little girl's mother spotted her chatting with Josh and came running towards them. Before she reached her daughter, the little girl planted her fist into Josh's hair. When her mother pulled her away, a big chunk of his hair went with them.

"Ouch," said Josh, rubbing his head. "That hurt."

An old man came up to Will. Their noses almost touched as he inspected Will's glasses. He carefully lifted them off his face, examined them, and grunted as he handed them back.

"I wonder what they do if they can't see properly? I'd be lost without my glasses," mused Will.

"There's not much they can do. I guess they manage the best they can," said Ellen.

Puma stopped in front of a small stone building just past the market area. "This is our home. We're not rich like the merchants, but our house is bigger than most because of our father."

"Do we get to meet him?" asked Ellen.

"Aawk," screeched Aqua from his perch on Luna's wrist. "Meet him. Meet him."

"That would be kind of hard," answered Luna sadly. "He's dead."

Ellen blushed furiously. "Oh, sorry. I didn't know. Why do I always say the wrong thing?"

"It's okay. Our father was a famous warrior and a great hunter. All of the animals trembled when they sensed his presence. Sit down for a minute, and I'll tell you about him," said Puma.

Everyone sat down on the little patch of grass in front of his home. Josh tried not to think about eating.

"A long time ago, when Luna was just a baby, our village was involved in a battle with the Chokolkas, Sharjay's tribe. They accused some of the men from our village of destroying their crops, and they tried to steal our herd of goats. One night they launched what they thought was a surprise attack against us, but we were prepared and fought back with great courage. The fighting was terrible. Just when it looked like our village would be overtaken, my father managed to sneak behind them. He single-handedly surprised them with his counterattack. They didn't know which way to go, in front or behind, and in all of the confusion our people won."

"Our father couldn't get back to the village, though. He was captured, tortured, and killed. The tribal council ordered that our mother be given this house as a way of saying thanks," said Luna.

Just then their mother appeared in the doorway. She was beautiful, with long dark hair braided flat against her head and lovely brown eyes. Luna looked just like her. "Children, who are your friends?" she asked softly.

"They have strange names—Josh, Will, and Ellen—and they are not from around here, but they are kind, Mother. I know you will like them," said Puma.

"Are you sick?" she asked.

Luna spoke up before they could answer. "No, Mother, they're not sick. They say everyone looks like them where they come from."

"Where are you from?"

"We're from a country called Canada. It would take days to get there from here. You could sail in a boat, but flying would be quicker," said Ellen.

"Flying, you say? I've never heard of anyone doing that. Is that how you arrived here?"

Josh stuck out his chest. "No. We came by some sort of magic."

"Josh, that's not true," protested Ellen.

"That's what the Shaman said."

Ellen glared at him, and then turned to Luna's mother. "I'm not sure how to explain our journey here. We came by a tunnel that disappeared once we were in the jungle. I hope it comes back so we can go home."

"Do you have a family?"

"Yes. Our mom and dad are probably worried sick by now."

"You know, ma'am, there is one thing I've been wondering. Where exactly are we?" asked Will.

"You are in the village of Quinaroo."

"Oh, so that's what it's called," said Josh.

"Quinaroo is located on an island surrounded by warm turquoise waters. Several other villages can be found on our island, but all are at least four days away. I have been told that there is a much bigger island across the water, but no one from our village has ever gone there and returned alive. They say it is inhabited by a fierce tribe of cannibals."

"I can see why no one wants to go there," agreed Josh.

"Would you like to join us for our midday meal?" she asked.

"That depends. You're not cannibals, are you?"

Ellen groaned. "What kind of question is that?"

"Don't you think we should check? What if they're planning to eat us for lunch?"

"There's no danger of that," said Puma. "You're way too

scrawny." Josh's jaw dropped and his eyes bugged out. "I'm just joking. Would you like some lunch?"

"Yes, please." Josh felt like he hadn't eaten in days.

Puma and Luna took them to the back of their house. A pot rested on a mound of hot coals in the courtyard. Luna bent over and stirred the warm grain mixture in the pot. It looked and smelled like oatmeal. A minute later her mother carried out a stack of wooden bowls. She filled each one with a scoop of the grains. Mugs of steaming hot cocoa completed the meal.

"Wow, this is great. Our mom never lets us drink hot chocolate at lunch. We have to stay outside for at least an hour in the winter before she'll even consider making any," said Josh.

"Everyone drinks it here. They say it will make you popular with the girls," advised Puma.

Josh cast his sister a sly glance. She was sitting beside him, quietly eating, minding her own business. "Ellen's always complaining about how everyone has a boyfriend except for her. Do you think hot chocolate would help her?"

"I don't know. She could give it a try," said Puma.

Ellen turned bright red.

"She'd probably have to drink five hundreds cups. She needs all the help she can get."

Ellen swatted Josh on the arm. "You're so mean," she said.

Puma's mother poked her head out the door before Josh could respond. "Puma, when you're done eating, why don't you take your friends out to see JoJo? You can bring some of my fresh bread with you."

"Who's JoJo?" asked Will.

A little smile passed between Puma and Luna. "Don't tell them. Let's make it a surprise," said Puma.

"What kind of answer is that? You told us not to be afraid to ask questions. The least you could do is give us a decent answer when we actually ask you one," said Josh.

Puma grinned. "Too bad. If you come, you might find out."

"But only if it's a good day," added Luna. "Don't worry. It's a nice surprise. Before we go, you need to change. We'll lend you some clothes so you can blend in a little better."

She found a dress for Ellen and a long strip of fabric for each of the boys. Ellen went inside to change and emerged a few minutes later in a long, colorful dress. Other than her fair skin and light brown hair, she looked like she had lived in the village all her life.

Josh held up his clothing for a closer inspection. "Hey, Puma, what's with this diaper thing? Is this the same thing everyone else here is wearing?"

"It's called a loincloth. It's like wearing a pair of shorts," said Ellen.

"Excuse me, but what do you know about boy's underwear? It's not like you've ever worn any before."

"It's not underwear, and in case you didn't notice, I read a lot. It's amazing what you can learn from books."

"That's nice, but if the basketball team saw me wearing this, they'd never let me forget it. There is no way I'm putting this on."

Ellen firmly squeezed his arm as she leaned over, and whispered in his ear. "You're embarrassing me and probably insulting Puma. Go put it on, NOW!"

Josh disappeared inside the house. Will reluctantly trailed behind. Muttering and complaining, a giggle, and an occasional burst of laughter drifted out the window, followed by the sound of one of the boys punching the other.

Will came out first, looking extremely uncomfortable. His skin was so white that the sun practically reflected off his chest. Josh strutted out behind him, making muscle poses. "Me Tarzan. Where Jane?" he quipped.

"I don't think this is any better than my dirty pajamas," complained Will.

"You don't know how good you've got it. That sure beats this long dress that I have to wear—not that I'm complaining." Ellen looked over at Luna. "It's very nice, and I'm happy to wear it; but I guarantee that by this afternoon, you'll be thankful you got to ditch your flannel pajamas."

"I wouldn't be caught dead wearing flannel pajamas. It's Will you're thinking of." Josh struck his teapot pose. "Hi, I'm Will," he said in a high-pitched voice, "and these are my fancy pajamas. Aren't they just so, so, so beautiful?"

"Back off," ordered Ellen. "We don't need another fight."

"It's not my fault. I'm not the one who wears fancy pajamas. I'm just a simple guy. I'll take my boxers and Dad's old T-shirts over Will's pretty pajamas any day."

"All right. You can wear whatever you want, and Will can wear whatever he wants, and we don't have to talk about it."

"Why do you have to make fun of me all the time, Josh? Just because I'm different than you doesn't mean that you're right and I'm wrong," sulked Will.

"I didn't say you were wrong. I just said you dressed funny."

"Did not."

"Did too. I don't know anyone else who wears ironed pants and shirts with buttons to school. In case you didn't notice, it's not like we go to a private school where we have to wear stuff like that."

"Josh, that's enough. You're making things worse," said Ellen.

"You're the one who started it. You're the one who said I wear fancy pajamas like Will, which I don't."

"Sorry. Now let it go, okay?"

"Okay."

"Puma and Luna are taking us back through the village. Just try to fit in, and please, no more arguing," she begged.

As they trekked through the village, Josh and his siblings still received some strange looks, but this time no one ran away. Luna had done a good job. They managed to fit in much better.

It was a perfect day for a walk. The temperature was warm but not too hot, a nice breeze kept the bugs away, and there was not a single cloud in the sky. They passed through an opening in the stone wall, walked down a well-worn path, and emerged onto a beautiful beach.

Soft sand stretched for miles. They quickly discovered it was a perfect place for shell collecting. Ellen's favorites were the pink conch shells that had floated in on the early morning tide. Josh liked the "kittens' paws" that littered the beach—tiny white and beige striped shells that looked like kittens' feet, claws and all.

Before long, he had a handful. From time to time they came across tidal pools full of small fish, sea urchins, and bits of seaweed.

A little ways ahead, Josh spotted a bright red cloud hovering over the water. "What's that?" he asked.

"Just a flock of flamingoes. They're there all the time," said Puma. As they got closer, Josh could make out the individual birds.

"Oh, they're beautiful. I wish we had some at home," said Ellen.

"They live on the sand bar," replied Puma.

"Do you have any idea how lucky you are to have a flock of flamingoes living nearby? That's totally amazing."

"It is?"

"We don't have anything like that at home. You're lucky to live in such a beautiful place."

"What about the Canada geese? They fly over our house," prompted Will.

"That's different—they aren't beautiful like flamingoes."

"I think they look nice when they fly by in those big 'v' formations."

"I suppose. I guess I'm just used to them, that's all."

"You still haven't told us who JoJo is. Is he your friend?" asked Josh.

Luna smiled. "Would you like to meet her?"

"She's a girl?" he exclaimed. "Great, now you tell me. I don't like hanging out with girls." He paused for a moment, and then realizing his mistake, he added, "except with you and Ellen, of course."

"If you want to meet JoJo, you'll have to get wet. Follow me," said Puma. He ran to the water, and yelled, "Last one in is a rotten coconut," before diving into the waves. The movement frightened the flamingoes, and the air filled with soaring red birds.

Will ducked down. "What are we supposed to do?" he whimpered.

"Join him?" suggested Ellen. She and Josh and Luna ran into the water after him.

"Wait for me," shouted Will after finding a safe place for his glasses.

He was about halfway to the others when a big wave started rolling in. Josh was farther out, and it reached him first. He swam a few strokes until it picked him up and carried him towards shore, growing bigger and bigger until it was tipped with frothy white foam. "Hey, look at me. I'm body surfing!" he shouted as he headed in his brother's direction.

Will turned around just in time to see the wave crest. He gasped and went under as it broke on top of him. Coughing and sputtering, he struggled to get his head back above the water. Suddenly a gray fin popped up behind him and began to circle him. "Help! Shark! It's trying to get me!" Will tried to dog paddle away, but the fish moved in closer. "Help!"

Josh quickly swam over to him. Will wrapped his arms around Josh's neck, and his legs around his waist. "Let go!" shouted Josh. "You're hurting me! I can't breathe."

"Save me, Josh! Save me!"

SEVEN

The Chosen One

Will's panic-stricken voice finally got Puma's attention, and he let out a low whistle. "JoJo, come here!" The large gray dolphin swam over to him and leaped out of the water, landing between him and Ellen with a splash. "Sorry about that. JoJo's such a showoff. She can't help herself," he explained.

Josh dragged his brother onto the shore. They sat down together and watched Ellen, Luna, and Puma frolic with JoJo out in the surf. "I don't believe it! This is incredible," said Josh. He stood up and put his hands around his mouth. "Puma, how come you get to drink hot chocolate for lunch and hang out with a dolphin all afternoon? Some people have all the luck!"

"Come back in," yelled Puma.

Josh looked over to his brother. "Do you mind if I go back?"

Will gave Josh a weak smile. "I'm okay as long as I'm on shore. How come you're being so nice to me? That's not like you."

Josh shrugged. "I suppose it's the right thing to do. What I said to you before about the way you dress—I shouldn't have said that." He picked up a handful of sand and let it dribble through his fingers. "I guess what I'm trying to say is ... well, you know ... sorry."

"It's all right. I probably shouldn't get so mad at you either. I know I'm different, but I can't help it. It's just the way I am. Sometimes its good, like when my teachers think I'm really smart because I wear nice clothes, but other times it makes me feel like a loser."

"I don't think you're a loser. Most of the time I'm glad you're my brother."

Will scrunched up his nose and smiled. "Thanks, I think."

Josh lightly punched him on the shoulder. Will punched back a little harder.

"You're sure you don't mind if I go in?" Josh asked again.

"You can do whatever you want as long as I can stay here."

"Okay. Thanks." Josh ran through the soft sand and dove back into the ocean.

"Come on, Will. Come join us," yelled Puma.

"No thanks. You can play without me."

JoJo loved to zip between them. Every few minutes she leaped out of the water, sometimes turning a somersault in midair. She even allowed Josh to hang on to her fin.

Josh was grinning from ear to ear as they swam by. "Look at me! I'm swimming with a dolphin," he shouted.

When everyone was tired out, they returned to the beach and ate a small meal of bread, goat cheese, and fresh water from the town well.

Josh settled underneath a palm tree. "You guys are so lucky. This place is amazing. This is definitely the best day of my life. I still can't believe I swam with a dolphin."

Will let out a big yawn. "Why do I feel so tired?"

"Probably from the excitement of your 'shark' attack. Don't you know the difference between a shark and a dolphin? They're completely different, you know," said Puma.

"Will might be smart at some things," replied Josh, "but …" He wiggled his chin back and forth as he considered what to say next. "You can't expect us to know everything about this place. We've never been here before, remember?"

"And you probably don't have dolphins where you live, right?" said Luna.

"All we have is some ugly old frogs in our pond. They're not nearly as exciting as your dolphins."

Ellen let out a big yawn. "All this fresh air and sunshine is making me sleepy. Do you mind if I take a nap?"

Before anyone could answer, she closed her eyes and fell fast asleep.

An hour later, everyone woke up. "Mmm," said Josh, stretching, "that felt good. Boy, did I ever need that."

Will's eyes flickered open for a brief minute before he rolled over onto his back.

Puma slowly got to his feet. "Don't move," he ordered.

"What?" Will started to sit up but stopped in mid-air. "Is there a wasp on me?"

Instead of answering, Puma jumped over him, spraying sand everywhere, and ran into the jungle. Josh could hear him thrashing through the bushes. A minute later he returned, proudly carrying a large iguana by the tail.

"Whatever that is, don't bring it near me. It looks terrible. Is that a miniature dinosaur or something?" asked Ellen.

"It's an iguana. My mother will be so pleased—she'll cook it for dinner," said Puma.

"You're feeding us a reptile for dinner? I don't think I can eat that," grumbled Will.

"Come on, guys, be good sports. If Puma's mom makes it, we should try it. It probably tastes like chicken," said Josh.

"Speak for yourself. You can have my share," offered Ellen.

"That's all right. You don't have to have any. My mother is also making turtle soup."

"Great, more wildlife. Just what I was hoping for," she muttered.

"If you like, I can save the head for you. It's my favorite part, but since you're our guest, I'd like you to have it."

Ellen grimaced. "Thanks, but after that big lunch, I'm not hungry. I won't be needing dinner tonight."

"You can decide later. You'll probably change your mind once you smell it. Come on, everybody, it's time to start back. I need to get this to my mother while it's still warm," said Puma.

As they walked along the beach, back to the village, Josh spotted someone sitting in the sand. "Who's that up ahead?" he asked.

"It's Onamee, the Shaman," said Puma.

"What's he doing out here on the beach?"

"He comes out here often."

"Do you think we could go back a different way? I don't want to see him again," said Ellen.

"Don't worry. There's no way you can get into trouble out here."

"That's what I thought before when we were standing by the temple, and look what happened: trouble. Big trouble. I don't want to go through that again."

"But it all turned out okay," said Josh.

"I know, but it was pretty scary at the time."

As they got closer to the Shaman, two little girls popped out of the water and scurried up the beach. They ran around and around him, shaking off like two little puppies that had just gone for a swim. As drops of water landed on him, he cringed, and the girls squealed with delight. One of them tripped in the sand, and he scooped her up into his strong arms, gave her a big hug, and then she wriggled out of his grasp and ran back to the water, ready to repeat the entire performance once again.

"Who are those kids? Do their parents realize who they're with?" asked Will.

"Those are Onamee's daughters. Aren't they cute? I look after them sometimes," said Luna.

"He has daughters? Who'd want to be his kid?" sneered Josh.

"What do you mean?"

"No offense, but I wouldn't want a Shaman for my dad. Look at him. He wears a jaguar tooth necklace, and he's covered in paint. You've got to admit, he looks pretty scary."

"His daughters don't think so. It's obvious they love playing with him."

As they walked by, the Shaman raised his hand in greeting. His daughters flailed themselves onto his lap, and the three of them fell back onto the sand.

"Who would have thought that someone actually loves him? That's too strange for words," said Ellen.

When they arrived back at the village, a large fire blazed in front of the temple. "Are we having a barbeque tonight? I could use a nice juicy cheeseburger right about now," suggested Josh.

"It's probably for cooking Puma's iguana. You're the one who volunteered to eat it, remember," said Will.

"Sorry to disappoint you all, but we won't be cooking anything on that fire tonight. I almost forgot, but tomorrow is the Ascension of the Sun ceremony," said Puma.

"What's that?" asked Ellen.

"Don't you have an Ascension of the Sun ceremony?" Ellen shook her head. "How could you miss such an important day?"

"Maybe we used to have one, but they stopped having it," suggested Josh.

"I don't think so. I've never heard of it before. Why is it important?" asked Will.

"It's the day when the sun shines on the carving of Cha at the top of the temple and casts a special shadow down the sides of the steps," explained Puma.

"Our village always makes a sacrifice, and sometimes a new priestess is chosen to serve in the temple. That way we will be sure to have good weather and rain for our crops," added Luna.

"Cha is the strongest and mightiest of the gods!" shouted Puma, pumping his hand in the air.

"If I hear that bit about Cha one more time, I think I'll scream. Imagine, worshiping a snake. That is so weird," whispered Ellen.

"You know, in church we learned about how people used to make sacrifices to our God, too. In the first part of the Bible, it was the only way they could get forgiveness for the things they had done wrong," said Will.

Puma looked puzzled. "What's a Bible?"

"You've never heard of the Bible?"

"No. What is it?"

"It's a book."

"What's a book?"

"Oh, brother. We're really starting at the beginning, aren't we?"

"The Bible is a collection of stories about our God. It tells us about him, how he wants us to live, about his Son Jesus, and all kinds of other stuff," said Ellen.

"What does your Bible say about your God?" asked Puma. Before Ellen could reply, he spotted his mother in their doorway, sobbing.

Puma ran over to her and grabbed her hand. "What's wrong, Mother? Are you hurt?"

"Oh, Puma," she moaned.

"Why are you crying? What's the matter?"

"It's your sister, Luna." She looked at her daughter, her eyes brimming with tears.

"Luna's been with me all day, Mother. I haven't let her out of my sight. She's fine."

"No, Puma, she is not fine."

A group of guards stepped out of Puma's home. Two of them grabbed Luna by the arms.

"What's going on? Onamee released Luna this morning. The death in Sharjay's village had nothing to do with her, and he knows it. Let go of her!" ordered Puma.

"Stop, my son. You're right—but this has nothing to do with Sharjay. Luna was … she was …"

One of the guards finished her sentence for her. "She was chosen."

"No! No! It can't be me! It must be a mistake. I'm not worthy!" shouted Luna. She strained towards her mother, but the guards held her firmly in place. "Mother, no! Stop them! Save me!"

"I'm sorry, daughter, but I can't." She walked over to Luna, and held her face in her hands. "Goodbye, my darling. I will always love you with all my heart."

"No, Mother, no! I'm not leaving you. I belong here with you and Puma. This must be a mistake."

The senior guard gently shook his head. "Luna, say your good-byes."

"But I'm not ready to go," she sobbed.

"Luna, you must fulfill your duty with dignity and honor. We've suspected for a while that you would be chosen. You're distressing everyone with your tears. Please go," said Puma.

Luna looked down at the ground as she contemplated his words. Then she looked up, tears pouring down her cheeks, and gave her mother the saddest look Josh had ever seen. The grief in her eyes was heartbreaking. She mouthed the words, "Good bye," and then she turned, and with a guard on either side, slowly walked to the temple, away from her home forever.

Puma let out a loud sob and fell down on his knees. He wrapped his arms around his mother's legs. "Oh, Mother, we have been honored. Cha is looking upon us with great favor. Our Cha is truly the strongest and mightiest of the gods."

"Yes, Puma, I know, but that doesn't make this any easier." She walked back into the house, sobbing.

"What's going on? What was your sister chosen for?" asked Ellen.

Will walked over to him, and patted him on the arm. "You know, Puma, where we live, some people want to be picked to be on student council and things like that. They get really upset if they don't get picked, but I've never heard of anyone being heartbroken because their kid was chosen. It's supposed to be a good thing to get chosen."

"Remember when I told you that we have an Ascension of the Sun ceremony?" said Puma.

Josh nodded. "Why do I have the feeling something bad is coming?"

Puma ignored him. "Some years ago, the Shaman decided that in addition to making a sacrifice, from time to time he would choose a special girl to serve in the temple as a priestess. The tribal council of elders chooses a girl from our village known for her beauty and kindness. She has the privilege of bringing honor to her family and our village by devoting her life to Cha and assisting Onamee with his duties in the temple. By doing this, she will bring good fortune to our village, and Cha will give us rain and sunshine for our crops.

"After the Ascension of the Sun ceremony, the girl is left in a special hut in the jungle, near the cenote, and she lives there alone for four seasons while she prepares herself for her duties. After the seasons have passed, she returns to the village and serves as a priestess for the rest of her life. She is not allowed to have friends or get married, and she must look away if she sees anyone from her family. She is not allowed to speak to or touch anyone because she is sacred."

Ellen stared at him, wide-eyed. "You can't be serious."

"I am completely serious." His chin began to quiver. "Luna was chosen to be that girl."

"That's not exactly student council," said Josh.

Will scowled at him. "You've got that right."

"Let me get this straight. You're telling me your sister is going to become a priestess so your village will have good weather for your crops?" Ellen's voice grew louder. "You're never going to be with Luna again, and you consider this an honor?"

"Of course it's an honor. My sister was chosen because she is beautiful and kind. I am proud of Luna and pleased that she is worthy of this position. It says a lot for my family."

"So what was the fire for?" said Will.

"It's a part of the ceremonies."

"What's that cenote thing you talked about?" asked Josh.

"It's a deep pool outside our village. Special water bubbles into it from an underground spring. We are forbidden to go there. Luna will stay in a nearby hut."

Ellen took a step closer to him." What happened last year at the Ascension of the Sun ceremony? Did some other girl get chosen back then?"

"Yes, another girl from our village was chosen, but she accidentally drowned."

"And how were your crops? Did you have a good harvest?"

"We had too much rain and most of our crops rotted in the fields. It's a good thing we stored maize, or our village would have been in real trouble. That's probably why Onamee chose Luna this year. We can't survive two bad harvests in a row."

"So last year's ceremony didn't work," said Ellen pointedly.

"No, it did work, but Cha became angry with us. Two men from our village broke the ancient traditions so Cha turned on us and sent the rain."

"I guess that's one way of looking at it, but I think your ceremony and this priestess thing is nonsense. Your god can't control the weather any more than you or I can, and that girl gave up her freedom, and her life, for nothing. You know, Puma, I feel so horrible just thinking about Luna and the terrible life she'll have as a priestess that I think I'm going to be sick. Let's get out of here, guys."

"Where are you going?"

"I don't know—probably somewhere far away from your stupid village. Your traditions are barbaric and disgusting," she added, before stomping off.

"It's getting late. Where are we supposed to sleep?" asked Will.

"Follow the path behind the temple. It will lead you to the beach. You can sleep there."

The boys caught up to Ellen and led her to the path Puma described. It ended abruptly behind the temple, but steep stairs had been cut into the side of the cliff, allowing people to travel to the beach below.

As Josh, Will, and Ellen slowly walked down the steps, a beautiful view unfolded before their eyes. It was a windless night, and the water shone like a sheet of turquoise glass. A full moon hung low in the sky, lighting up the jungle and casting a long golden shadow across the sea. Deep in the water they could see a large fish gliding quietly along. The white sand beach lay below them, lined with tall palm and coconut trees. Every now and then they heard a bird cry out and another one answer its call.

Josh jumped when Puma suddenly appeared behind them. "I just wanted to make sure you were okay. Follow the steps down to the beach. It's the second best spot in the whole village to sleep—it almost beats my hammock."

Once they reached the sand, the breeze picked up. It was just enough to keep the mosquitoes away. Josh, Will, and Ellen snuggled together under one of the palm trees, trying to stay warm.

"Ellen, what are we going to do? We can't just sit around and wait while they ruin Luna's life," said Josh.

"I know. We have to do something. I just don't know what."

"Maybe things will seem better in the morning. That's what Mom always says," said Will.

Ellen rubbed her eyes. "I hope so."

"Me, too."

Within minutes they were all sound asleep.

Run for Your Life!

The sun was just peeking over the horizon when the squawking of a seagull woke Josh up. He rubbed his eyes. "It can't be time to get up already."

Will woke up next. Josh took one look at him and howled with laughter. "Ellen, wake up! Quick! Will's covered in bird poop."

"Get it off of me!" Will screamed.

"Calm down. It's no big deal. You'll be okay. Of all the people to get dirty, it would have to be you," chuckled Ellen. "Don't worry, you'll survive."

"Thanks for the sympathy." Will ran down the beach and knelt at the water's edge, scrubbing his face and arms.

Ellen pointed to a pair of seagulls patrolling the beach. "Look, there are the culprits. They're just looking for breakfast." Will joined them back under the palm trees, and they watched as one of the gulls landed beside a dead fish that had washed up during the night and devoured its remains.

"I feel like I swallowed a truck load of sand," said Josh.

"Maybe now you'll listen to me when I tell you not to sleep with your mouth open. Maybe a bird pooped in your mouth while you were sleeping," said Will.

"Don't be mean. Let's go for a swim. Last one in is a rotten coconut," shouted Ellen. The three of them ran down the beach together. Josh and Ellen dove into the warm ocean, and Will cautiously walked in after them.

Josh floated in the water near his brother and sister. "This is like being in the world's biggest bathtub. I wish we could have a bath like this every morning."

"If Mom and Dad were here, it would be perfect. I miss them. Do you think they're okay?" asked Will.

"They're fine. I just hope they're not mad at us for being gone so long," said Ellen.

A movement in the water caught Josh's eye. "Um, guys, do you see what I see?"

Ellen rolled out of her back float and began to tread water. "Did you say something?"

All the color had drained from Josh's face. "Check it out at four o'clock." Off to his right, two large fins glided back and forth in the water.

"Oh no," groaned Ellen. Two large gray fish slowly swam towards them. "Stay calm. Will, don't panic. You can touch bottom here. Walk back to shore."

They slowly backed up, their eyes never leaving the unwelcome visitors. The sharks slowly followed them in, coming so close that Josh could see their beady little eyes. When his heels finally hit the edge of the shore, he collapsed backwards onto the sand. "Whew! We made it."

"How did you know what to do, Ellen? You saved us," said Will, gratefully.

"I read somewhere that if you see a shark you should get out of the water as quickly as possible without causing too much commotion."

Josh pondered that thought for a moment. "Maybe I should read more."

"Did that really happen, or am I dreaming? I thought stuff like that only happened in the movies," said Will.

Ellen nodded. "An awful lot of strange things have happened to us since we got here. I'm starting to think we must have amazing guardian angels. Let's go find Puma. I feel safer when he's around."

She and the boys climbed back up the cliff and walked through the village. A few people stared, but it wasn't nearly as bad as the day before.

They had just passed a row of goats, tethered to some stakes in the ground, when Josh spotted Puma. "There he is. I'll race you to him."

"No, don't! Remember?" said Will.

"Remember what?"

"Today is the day Luna's going to become a priestess. We shouldn't bug him. He might still be upset."

Instead of running, the boys slowly walked to Puma's house and sat down beside him. Ellen stood a little ways away.

"Aren't you coming?" asked Josh.

"No, I'll stay here."

"Ellen, please come," urged Puma, in a quiet, forlorn voice. She reluctantly walked over to him. "Did you sleep okay?" he asked.

Ellen sighed. "It was hard to sleep after everything that's happened. I had terrible dreams about Luna all night. I'm not sure I want anything to do with your village."

"But, Ellen, I thought we were friends."

"We are friends, but I don't understand how you can just sit back and let this happen." She wiped a tear off her cheek. "Just think about it, this is your sister we're talking about. After tonight you are never going to be with her again. Doesn't that bother you?"

"Of course it bothers me. My mother and I didn't sleep all night. I'm really worried about her. First, my father dies protecting our village, and now …" He paused, unable to go on, and then in a voice so sorrowful that it broke Josh's heart, he continued. "And now my sister, she'll be taken away, too." He hung his head. Loud sobs wracked his chest.

Josh looked over to his brother. "What are we supposed to do?" Will shrugged his shoulders. Josh looked down at the bracelet around his wrist, the one his Sunday school teacher had given him for Christmas with the letters "WWJD" embroidered across it. He hesitated for a moment, and then reached over and gave Puma a big hug. Will and Ellen quickly joined in.

After Puma calmed down, he went inside and retrieved a basket of food. They walked back to the beach, and he spread out their breakfast on the sand: tortillas filled with cooked beans and shredded meat, and some sweet orange fruit, different than any they had ever tasted before.

"Here, Ellen," said Puma, handing her a tortilla. He carefully pressed the sides together so the filling wouldn't fall out. "I made this just for you. There's no meat in it."

Ellen blushed. "Thanks. That's so nice."

Josh leaned over to his brother. "I think she likes him," he whispered.

"Don't say anything, or she'll get really mad at you," said Will.

"Okay, I won't, for now."

A family of monkeys appeared on top of a nearby palm tree, chattering away. They swung from branch to branch with ease. The father monkey dangled upside down by his tail as he eyed their breakfast.

"I think they want to eat with us," said Josh.

"Don't even think about feeding them, because if you do, they'll never leave us alone," advised Puma.

As they sat there, quietly enjoying their breakfast, the sun began to heat up the sand. Everything around them glowed with life.

"I wonder if Mom and Dad are worried about us. I hope they haven't started a search party yet. Knowing Mom, she'll have our faces on every milk carton in the country by now. I can just see it: 'Wanted: Three Missing MacKenzies. Reward offered,'" said Ellen.

"Speaking of Mom, this fruit is sure good. We should ask her to buy some. Our fruit isn't nearly as tasty as this," mused Josh.

Will let out a feeble cough. "It might have something to do with the fact that we don't exactly have orange trees growing in our backyard."

"Do you think I don't know that? I'm not stupid."

"Oh, really?"

Josh ignored him. "Mom's a great cook and everything, but our food tastes completely different. It doesn't have any flavor compared to this stuff."

"Why does your food taste different?" asked Puma. He grabbed a little caterpillar that was crawling along the edge of the sand and popped it into his mouth.

"Did you see that? Puma just ate a live bug!" shrieked Will.

"Are you serious?" asked Josh.

"That's why his food tastes different. He eats it while it's still alive."

"Caterpillars are delicious. Here, try one," said Puma.

"I think we'll pass," stammered Ellen. She put her hand over her mouth so she wouldn't gag.

Puma gave her a concerned look. "Why is she acting so strange?"

"Don't ask. She's got some weird ideas about food. They usually don't make sense," explained Josh.

"Don't take it personally," added Will.

"You know, no one ever answered Puma's question. Why does our food taste different than his food?" asked Josh.

"Maybe it's because we cook it differently. We don't have a fire in our yard, so our bread doesn't have that smoky taste," said Will. He looked over at Puma. "We buy most of our bread at the grocery store. Our mom doesn't bake very often."

"What's a grocery store?"

"It's a place that sells food. They sell everything: potato chips, pop, candy, ice cream…. You name it, they sell it," explained Josh.

"Aren't you forgetting something?" said Will.

"Like what?"

"The four food groups—you know—bread, fruit and vegetables, meat, and dairy."

"I was just thinking of the good stuff."

"If we need fruit, we just go to a tree and pick it. Did you know there's a fruit tree right behind you?" asked Puma.

Josh's eyes lit up. "No way. Can you show me?" He followed Puma through the underbrush. Puma climbed the tree and threw down ten oranges, one at a time, and then they headed back to the beach, their arms loaded with sweet, plump fruit.

Josh wiped a sticky trickle of juice off his chin. "These are sure good! You were right, Puma. You don't need a store here. Why go to a store when you can pick your food yourself?"

"I wasn't going to try your oranges, but I'm glad I did. I usually like dehydrated fruit best. Fruit bars are good, but your oranges beat them any day. It must be nice to grow all your own food. I can tell you manage really well, considering you don't have electricity," observed Will.

"What's that?" asked Puma.

"It's kind of hard to explain. It's something we use to cook our food, light up our houses, and run our clocks so we can tell time."

"You know, we cook our food and light up our houses and tell the time without any of that electricity stuff."

"How do you play video games?" asked Josh.

"What's that?"

"Don't ask," answered Will. "You're right, Puma, you manage just fine. You have lots to eat, the sun lights up your village during the day, and I bet you go to sleep when it goes down for the night."

"And we know its time to get up when the sun rises again in the morning."

"In some ways, you're a lot smarter than we are," said Ellen.

Puma began to tidy up the remains of their meal. "I'm learning a lot from you. It sounds like the place you live is very different from Quinaroo. Can you tell me more about that nook you mentioned yesterday?"

"Nook? What nook?" asked Josh.

"You know, that nook that talks about your God."

Ellen frowned. "What's he talking about?"

"I think he means book. We were telling him about the Bible, remember?" said Will.

"Yes, that's the word, book. Tell me more about it."

"Well, the Bible is a book that explains what we believe. It talks about how God made the world and how people have lived in it ever since," explained Ellen.

"In the first part of the Bible, the people had to make sacrifices to God just like you do to Cha. I guess you're not that strange after all," said Josh.

Ellen elbowed him in the side. "Be polite."

"Just ignore my brother," said Will. "Back when the Old

Testament was written, sacrifices were the only way the people could get forgiveness for the things they did wrong. We could tell you hundreds of stories from the Bible, but it would take us days. The most important thing in the Bible is the story about Jesus. God saw how hard it was for his people to obey him, so he sent a special person, his Son, to earth."

"You know, I've always wished I could have met Jesus. I bet he was a really amazing guy. He traveled all over and told people about God and how much he loved them and how they were supposed to be good to each other," added Josh.

"You obviously weren't remembering that 'be good to each other' part this morning when you laughed at the bird poop on my face," sulked Will.

Josh shrugged. "Nobody's perfect."

"Anyway, getting back to our story, Jesus taught us that God wants to be our friend. He's not scary like your god. Our God loves us, and it makes him happy when we love him back," said Ellen.

Josh leaned forward, not wanting to miss this opportunity. "This guy, Jesus—he really was God. People didn't like the things he said because they were different than what the priests taught in the temple. Jesus said that if someone hits you, you should turn and let them hit you again instead of hitting back. Most of the things he taught were like that. They were the opposite of what you'd want to do."

"He did incredible things that no one had ever done before. He healed people who were sick; he raised a young girl from the dead; and one time he even fed five thousand people with just a few loaves of bread and fish," explained Will.

"The leaders were scared of him, so they arrested him and nailed him onto two big pieces of wood called a cross." Ellen drew an outline of a cross in the sand. "He died hanging on that cross, and they buried him. Three days later God brought him back to life.

God sent Jesus to be a gigantic one-time sacrifice so that people would never have to make sacrifices again. Isn't that amazing? Our God loves us so much that he sacrificed his own Son. That's the best kind of sacrifice you can get. Jesus' death cancelled out all the things we've done wrong and all the things we'll ever do wrong in the future."

"I can't imagine having a god who loves me. Cha's not like that. Onamee is always telling us about the evil tricks he played on our ancestors. He'd make them get sick or get lost in the jungle and die. Cha hurts us if we don't obey the Shaman. That's why Luna has to be a priestess. If we didn't do things like that, Cha would punish us. You're lucky your God loves you instead of getting angry at you all the time," said Puma.

"You know, you don't have to live like that. Our God loves everybody, even you and your village. Why don't you give him a chance?" asked Ellen.

"We'd better not talk about this any more. If the Shaman heard what you just said, you three would be thrown into the cenote and left to drown. That's the last thing I want to happen."

"All right, but if you change your mind, just let us know. We'd be happy to talk to you about this any time, right guys?"

"I don't know. I don't want to drown," protested Will.

Suddenly a group of warriors came running down the steps in the side of the cliff. Their faces were striped with green and black paint, and they carried long blowguns. Little pouches of poison darts hung around their necks. As they ran, they chanted, "May coo unoma…. May coo unoma."

"They must have heard us talking. They're coming to get us. Run for your lives!" shouted Will.

NINE

The Secret Path

Josh and Will sprinted down the beach, away from the warriors. "Guys, don't go! We haven't done anything wrong," yelled Ellen.

Josh stopped and looked back. The warriors were almost up to her. "Keep running," he hollered.

As the warriors passed Ellen and Puma, several of the men raised their hands in greeting. Ellen stood there, acting as if nothing unusual was happening. The warriors continued on down the beach. When they were almost even with the boys, they veered off into the jungle.

Josh skidded to a stop, but Will kept running along aimlessly. When he finally stopped and bent over, struggling to catch his breath, he heard Josh shout, "It's safe to come back now."

They walked back to Puma and Ellen. "Whew. That was a close call," said Josh.

Puma burst out laughing. "It sure was. It's not every day you meet a pack of hunters on the way to their hunting grounds."

"Hunters?" said Will incredulously. "They were going hunting? I thought they were coming to get us."

Puma smiled. "Sorry to disappoint you, but you weren't the main attraction. Maybe next time." He wandered down the beach by himself.

Ellen sat back down on the sand with her brothers. "I don't know about you guys, but there's no way I'm sitting around, waiting for the Shaman to ruin Luna's life forever."

"You're right. We have to do something," agreed Josh.

"Let's get Puma to take us to the cenote. Maybe once we see it we'll figure how to rescue her. Will, you ask him," said Ellen.

"Why me? I don't want to go there."

"If I ask him, he's going to be suspicious. He's more likely to say yes to you."

"But I'm not a good swimmer. Remember?"

"I promise I won't let you drown."

"Okay, but there's no guarantee he'll cooperate. Come on, Josh, let's go." They trudged down the beach together until they found Puma sitting at the edge of the water, watching the waves lap against his feet.

"What are you doing?" asked Will.

"Just thinking."

"About what?"

"I don't know. My sister, the village, lots of things."

"Do you think you could show us the cenote? We've never seen one before."

"I can't do that."

"I probably wouldn't want to go there either if I were you," agreed Josh.

"It's not just that. It's that the cenote is off limits to everyone but the Shaman. It's sacred territory. No one else is supposed to go there."

"Too bad. We really wanted to see it," said Will.

Puma sat there for a minute. "I'll tell you what. I'll take you if you promise not to tell anyone. I'll be in big trouble if Onamee finds out."

"You've got a deal." Josh grabbed his hand and shook it up and down.

Puma gave him a funny look. "What are you doing that for?"

"That's what we do in Canada when we make a deal—we shake on it. Come on, let's go!"

The four of them were walking down the beach when Puma suddenly plunged into the dense bush that was running alongside the sand.

"Where'd he go?" asked Josh.

Ellen pushed some branches to one side. "We'd better crawl in after him before we lose him."

Josh went first. He was barely into the bush when he spied a wide path, almost like a highway, that led deep into the jungle. Puma stood off to one side, waiting patiently for them to join him.

"Wow! This is amazing. We'd never have found this path without you. Why did you dive in like that?" said Josh.

"That's what we do when we want to keep something a secret. If our enemies mount a surprise attack, we have an extra way out. The main entrance to the path is located in the village."

"What a good idea," said Ellen.

"Come on. We need to keep moving. If we stay in one place too long, we're more likely to get caught."

As they trudged along in the muggy heat, Josh started to feel uneasy. He couldn't shake the funny feeling in the pit of his stomach. "Ellen, do you feel okay?" he asked.

"I'm starting to feel claustrophobic. Is it my imagination, or is this path getting narrower?"

"It just feels like that after being on the beach. There's not much of a breeze in here," said Puma.

A canopy of leaves blocked the sunlight. Every so often, a sunbeam managed to break through the trees, illuminating the hundred different shades of green around them. As they walked along, Puma pointed out the many varieties of trees and tropical flowers. Palm, banana, and breadfruit trees grew quickly in the damp soil. He bent over and picked a cluster of yellow berries off a low bush. Everyone tried some. They were juicy and sweet. Ferns as tall as a person sprung up from the jungle floor, and grass and delicate orchids lined the path.

"The village healer comes out here to select the plants for her medicine. She collects them, dries them, and stores them until she needs them," he said.

Suddenly Ellen stopped and plugged her nose. "Puma, stop for a minute. I just smelled something really bad."

"Yuck. It stinks like dead fish. Did something die out here or what?" complained Josh.

"See that giant lily over there? It puts out a scent that smells like rotten meat to attract the bugs it feeds on. We also have plants that eat small animals. Do you have those where you live?"

"All we have are some boring old oak trees and a few evergreens. The oak trees drop acorns all over our yard every fall, and for some unknown reason, I have to clean them up. Raking is the worst job," grumbled Will.

"No way. Cleaning toilets and washing the kitchen floor are way worse," insisted Josh. "Quit complaining."

"That's enough, guys. Be quiet so I can listen to Puma," said Ellen.

"What do oak trees look like?" he asked.

"They have rough bark, long bumpy leaves, and they make those nuts Will was just talking about," replied Josh.

"You should be thankful for the acorns. They feed the squirrels, you know," reminded Ellen.

"Did you know than an oak tree doesn't make acorns until it's at least twenty years old?" said Will, in his most authoritative voice. "Sometimes it takes even longer—up to fifty years. And squirrels aren't the only animals that eat acorns. Blue jays, woodpeckers, and wild turkeys like them too."

"Oh, brother," muttered Josh. "Where'd you learn all that?"

"I did a project on oak trees for school last year. They're actually a member of the beech family."

Josh caught Puma's eye. "Little Willy over there thinks he's a real genius, but don't let him fool you. He might know a lot, but he's actually pretty stupid sometimes."

A hint of a smirk flashed across Puma's face. "You two don't get along very well, do you?"

"We do when he's not trying to impersonate Albert Einstein." Puma gave Josh a puzzled look. "Don't ask. You don't want to know."

He and Puma walked along in a comfortable silence. Ellen and Will followed a few steps behind. "You know, those oak trees you were talking about before don't sound boring at all. I bet they're beautiful."

Josh pondered the thought for a minute. "I suppose. I like watching the squirrels climb the one in our backyard, and it looks especially nice when the new leaves come out in spring. Ours has this one perfect branch—it's really thick and just the right height from the ground—and we have a huge tire swing on it that can hold four people." He ran his fingers through his bangs. "Maybe they aren't so boring after all."

Suddenly Josh heard a strange rumbling noise, and the ground started to tremble.

"It's a herd of wild pigs. Get out of the way—NOW!" shouted Puma. He turned and grabbed Ellen and Will; they scrambled to one side of the path and climbed up a nearby tree. Josh ran to the other side, turned, and watched a large herd of white-lipped pigs thunder towards him.

"Climb the tree or you'll get trampled!" yelled Puma.

The pigs were getting closer and closer. Josh tried to climb the nearest tree, but he couldn't get a grip because of the slippery moss growing on its trunk. He looked up at Puma, his face a mask of fear. "What should I do?"

"Hang on. I'm coming!"

The pigs were only seconds away. As they ran down the path, clumps of dirt and rotting leaves floated in the air in their wake. Puma grabbed a long vine and swung over to Josh, grabbing him just before the pigs reached him. The vine was strong, but it stretched like a giant rubber band; so as they swayed back and forth over the path, they bounced up and down. They had to climb farther up it to avoid being trampled.

"Is this thing strong enough to hold both of us?" shouted Josh above the deafening roar.

"It's working so far, isn't it?"

"What's it tied to?"

"Look up," replied Puma.

High in the treetops, the vine had wound its way around the trunk of a tall, stately tree. When Josh looked back down, he saw the last of the pigs disappear down the path. "Whew. That was a close call."

"It definitely was, unlike your earlier episode with the hunters.

You really could use some climbing lessons. Remind me to teach you later."

"What are you talking about? That trunk was slippery. I couldn't get a grip."

"Oh, really?" said Puma. They slid down the vine, and he walked over to the tree in question. In one smooth motion he was halfway up the trunk.

"I … well … it didn't work like that for me," sputtered Josh.

Ellen and Will joined them. "And I thought you were the athletic one," said Will.

Ellen shot Will a dirty look. "It's all right, Josh. By the time Puma's through with you, you'll be the next Tarzan."

The group had safely resumed their trek down the path when Puma stopped and put his finger to his lips. "Shh." He motioned for everyone to follow him off the path into the jungle. They stepped over tree seedlings, around bushes and vines, and crouched in a deep layer of fallen leaves. Puma put his finger to his lips again and pointed to something behind a massive tree trunk.

Ellen crept over and peered around the trunk first. Just past the leaves in front of her she could see an opening in the ground. It looked like a meteor had landed, creating an enormous hole. A young boy walked ahead of the Shaman as he circled the hole, picking up the branches and palm fronds that littered their path. As the Shaman moved he waved his spindly walking stick in front of him. He stopped every few steps, took something out of the pouch tied around his waist, and sprinkled it onto the ground.

Ellen turned back to the group. "Is that the cenote?"

Puma nodded.

"It's just a big hole."

"It may look like just a hole, but it's dangerous. It drops the height of ten men before you even reach water."

"Let me see," exclaimed Josh, pushing his way past Ellen. His foot caught on a tree root, and he tripped and fell to the ground. Blood gushed out of his nose. "I don't believe it. Just what I need, a nosebleed in the middle of the jungle," he whined.

"Be quiet. They're going to see us!" whispered Puma.

The Shaman stopped, said something to the boy with him, and pointed in Josh's direction. The boy ran straight to the spot where they were hiding and looked directly at them. Josh stood there, completely motionless, blood dripping from his nose, as the boy stared at him. Finally he looked at Puma, put his finger to his lips, and returned to the Shaman.

"I think we're okay. I know him. If we're quiet he won't give us away. That means you, Josh," ordered Puma.

They waited patiently for the Shaman to finish his walk around the cenote. He circled the hole seven times, closed up his pouch, and then he and his helper walked away, down the path that led to the village.

Puma breathed a sigh of relief. "That was nerve-wracking. I don't want to go through that again."

"Look! They're coming back," whispered Will.

"Oh no. We've been caught!"

TEN

The Cenote

████████████████████████████████

The Shaman stopped near their hiding spot. His eyes narrowed to tiny slits as he peered into the jungle. A shiver ran up and down Josh's spine as he stared right where they were hiding. Finally, after what seemed like hours, he turned and walked away.

Josh breathed a sigh of relief. "Whew. That was a close one. Thank you, God."

"Your God must have been looking after us, because Cha would have revealed our hiding place to Onamee," said Puma.

Ellen cringed. "Just seeing him made my skin crawl. He is so evil."

"He's not evil. His magic is good."

"I don't know how to break this to you, but Onamee is not a good guy," warned Ellen.

"Why would you say that? He's done so many good things for my village. Besides, what has he ever done to hurt you? He let you go after you were caught. You should be thankful for that."

"I don't know how to explain it, but I just know in my heart that he's bad."

"I know what you mean," said Josh. "One time when I was over at my friend's house, I put on this fancy necklace, and these really weird pictures kept coming into my head. When I took it off, the pictures stopped. Later I asked my friend about it, and he told me that his older brother bought the necklace from a witch doctor he met when he was in Africa," said Josh.

"That's creepy," said Will.

"It was scary."

"How come you never told me about that before?"

"It was too strange to talk about. I told you now only because I agree with what Ellen said. Sometimes our hearts just know when something isn't right."

Everyone stared at Josh. He stuck out his chest and tried to look serious.

"So, when exactly did this happen to you?" said Ellen.

"I don't remember. Maybe a year ago."

"That's interesting, because there's a magazine lying on the living room coffee table that has a story of a teenager who had that exact experience you just described. The only difference is that he trashed his house before his parents figured out what the necklace was doing to him."

"Really?"

"Yes, really."

"Oh." Josh stood there, shifting his weight back and forth from one foot to the other.

"It's wrong to lie, Josh, but I shouldn't have to tell you that. You already know that."

"Maybe I was just confused."

"It's wrong to lie," insisted Ellen.

"Whatever," he sneered. He struck his teapot pose. "Hi, I'm Super Ellen, the lie detector princess. You can count on me to sniff out any hint of trouble, because I know everything."

"You're the one with the problem, not Ellen. It's not her fault you got caught," declared Will.

"Come on. The coast is clear. Let's get this over with," said Puma.

Large craggy rocks surrounded the cenote, and gnarled trees grew out of its sides. Despite its rustic beauty, there was an evil feeling to the place.

A hawk glided over the still green water. Ellen walked up to a small stone building on one side and stopped on the platform in front of it. "Is this where Luna will stay?"

"Yes," said Puma. He scrunched his eyes shut. "I don't want to think about it."

Ellen put her hand on his shoulder. "Everything will be okay."

Puma jerked away. "No, everything will not be okay. My sister is going to be abandoned here tonight, and there's nothing I can do about it. If I stay here any longer, I'm going to go crazy." He backed away from the platform. "Keep your eyes open for crocodiles. Trust me, you don't want to run into one of them," he warned, before disappearing into the jungle.

Josh crept over to Ellen and looked over the edge of the platform. "Wow, it looks deep," he said.

Ellen picked up a small stone and dropped it over the edge. There was a long pause before they heard a sharp splash in the water below. "They should put a fence around this place. You wouldn't want to go for an unexpected swim."

They walked back to Will, who was standing on the path that circled the cenote. "Let's take a look around, but be careful. If you fall in, there's no way I can get you out. So much for rescuing Luna," said Ellen.

Puma stepped out from behind a nearby bush. "What are you talking about?"

"I thought you had left."

"I came back to keep an eye on you. What were you saying about Luna?"

"It's obvious you're upset that she was chosen to be a priestess. We thought we'd try to help by rescuing her. I'm not sure how to help her, though, so I thought if we could see the cenote, I might get some ideas. I'm sure something will come to me."

"What are you thinking? I'm not happy Luna was chosen, but I know it happened for a reason, and it has to be done. It's an honor for her to serve as a priestess, and besides, if you go anywhere near her, the guards will kill you."

"Sorry. I was just trying to help."

"Well, that's not the kind of help I need." Puma spun around and stalked off. They tried to catch up, but he moved so quickly that he was soon out of sight.

The three of them huddled in the middle of the path. "I don't want to get Puma into trouble, but this is our only chance to work out a rescue mission. Let's go scout out the area around the cenote some more. Hopefully we can come up with a plan," said Ellen.

Will shook his head. "You heard Puma. He doesn't want our help."

A look of determination crossed Ellen's face. "As far as I'm concerned, we don't have a choice. If I don't help Luna, I know I'll regret it for the rest of my life."

The search around the cenote turned up a few vines, a slimy moss-covered log, two red-spotted toads, and not much else.

"I've got an idea. How about we wind some vines into a nice

strong rope and tie up the Shaman?" said Josh.

"What good would that do? The guards would arrest us. There's only three of us and a million of them," griped Will.

"There are not a million guards. There's only forty or fifty."

"Still, I'm not volunteering to help fight them off."

"That's fine with me, because I've got a better idea. How about we make a rope, tie it onto a tree, and then when the guards aren't looking, we can swing down, grab Luna, and swing back into the jungle on the other side? I've swung on vines. It's not that hard," maintained Josh.

"I don't believe it. This is coming from the guy who couldn't even climb a tree when he was being chased by a herd of wild pigs. Joshua Donald MacKenzie, you're something else," said Ellen.

"I was on a vine with Puma. It wasn't that hard."

Will cleared his throat. "You would have been trampled if he hadn't saved you."

"I'd like to see you try swinging on a vine. You'd fall off for sure."

"Whatever."

"You obviously haven't noticed that most of the trees and bushes around the cenote have been cleared away. There's not a tree close enough to use. Besides, I don't think we could make a rope that would be long enough. I think the real problem is that we're out-numbered," said Ellen.

"And it would be kind of hard to hide from the guards," added Will.

"Hang on. I've got an idea. How about we rig up a little plane? Then we could fly in, grab Luna, and fly back out." Josh thumped his thumb against his chest. "I know. I'm brilliant."

"And where exactly are you going to get the parts to make this little plane of yours? Besides, I'm positive you don't exactly have a set of do-it-yourself airplane instructions kicking around in your back pocket," said Will.

Josh stuck out his tongue at him. "Maybe Uncle Vic could come in his helicopter. If he was here, he could lower a basket and Luna could jump in. Can you imagine how scared those villagers would be if a helicopter showed up in the middle of their jungle?"

"Guys, come on, focus! This is Luna's life we're talking about. We have to be serious about this," insisted Ellen.

"All right, but do you have to be so bossy?" muttered Josh.

"I'm not bossy. Someone has to be in charge. I think it's impossible for us to help Luna out here in the jungle. That means there's only one solution: we need to rescue her before they bring her out here."

"You mean, like kidnap her or something?" said Josh, his eyes gleaming.

"I never thought of it that way, but that's what we need to do. We need to kidnap her!" exclaimed Ellen.

"That sounds dangerous. Couldn't we go to jail for that?" asked Will.

"They probably don't have jails here, so why worry about it? Let's go find her," said Josh.

Ellen straightened up. "Now you're talking. I know exactly where she is. This will be a piece of cake."

The three of them bounded down the path that led to the village. "We're going on a mission. We're going on a mission," said Josh in a singsong voice.

"Calm down. It's probably not going to be as easy as you think," said Will.

"What do you mean?"

"Just keep thinking those happy thoughts, because I have a feeling we're going to need them."

Once they got closer to the village, they stayed near the edge of the path so they could duck into the jungle if anyone unexpected came along. They were almost at the village when the path ahead of them suddenly grew dark.

"What's that?" asked Josh. He bent down to take a closer look, and suddenly his legs were covered with a swarming mass of ants. "Ouch!" he yelled as he jumped up and down, shaking his legs. "Stay back! Killer ants!"

Will and Ellen quickly backed up and managed to avoid them. Josh did a crazy little dance in front of them as he struggled to get the nasty critters off his legs. Finally Ellen came over and helped him brush them off. "I think we've got them all, but look at your skin. It's turning red and splotchy. Are you okay?"

"I think so, but my legs really hurt. Ant bites are way worse than bee stings."

"What are we going to do? There must be thousands of ants over there. We could be here for hours," said Will.

"We may as well sit down and wait. There's not much else we can do," said Ellen.

They found a comfortable spot, a respectable distance from the ants, and sat down in the shade. After waiting for what seemed like forever, all three of them fell asleep.

Ellen woke up first. "Come on, guys. The ants are gone. Let's go."

Josh lifted his arms up and stretched. "Boy, that felt good. I didn't know I was that tired."

"We're almost at the village. Before we go, there are two things you need to remember. First, Puma warned us that we could be in danger here. If we look like we know what we're doing, people will assume that everything is okay. So try to look confident, okay?" The boys nodded in agreement. "Second, it's critical that we stick together. If we get separated, I don't know if I could find you again. So whatever you do, stay close to me."

"We'll stick to you like glue," said Josh.

"Good. Let's go."

Ellen strode confidently through the village with the boys following close behind. Even though Josh desperately wanted to look around, he kept his eyes focused straight ahead so he wouldn't lose her. They walked past the field workers' huts, the house of the healer, and the group of stone buildings where Puma and his family lived, before continuing on through a small courtyard filled with colorful flowers. Several villagers sat on a log overlooking the ocean. They glanced up as Ellen and the boys walked by, but quickly resumed their conversation.

As they approached the temple, Ellen veered off the stone path and hid behind a clump of banana trees. Josh and Will scooted in behind. They crouched down beside her and watched as she drew a map in the dirt with her finger.

"This is where we are," she said, pointing to one spot, "and straight ahead of us is the hut where we slept the first night," she said, pointing to another. "This is where it gets tricky. Puma told me that Luna will be in that hut until the ceremony begins. They keep their priestess away from everyone else while they do some special chanting and stuff. We need to creep up, sneak in, and quietly grab her before anyone notices. Are you with me?"

"I'm with you," said Josh.

"I'll try," stammered Will. He hugged his arms against his chest, but he couldn't stop shaking.

"Are you ready?" asked Ellen.

"Ready," replied Josh.

"Good. Follow me."

Ellen crouched over and ran to the hut. She motioned for her brothers to follow. They caught up to her, and the three of them crept toward the doorway. Everything was going according to plan. They were about to enter the hut, when suddenly Josh was lifted off the ground.

"No! Put me down! Let me go!"

— ELEVEN —

The Shaman's Lair

Josh clawed at the hands around his waist. Using every ounce of strength he possessed, he dug his fingernails in as hard as he could. Nothing happened. "Put me down!" he yelled again.

As quickly as he had been picked up, he was let go, and he landed on the ground with a thud. An enormous warrior with arms and legs as thick as tree trunks stood over him. Will landed on Josh's right, and then Ellen followed on his left.

The three guards stared down at them. "It happens every time," muttered one.

"I don't know why they even bother. They're no match for us," said one of the others.

"We don't need any problems tonight. Get out of here, or you'll live to regret it!" said the tallest one. They turned and walked back to the hut.

Will brushed himself off. "So much for that idea. Did you see their muscles? They could have squashed us with their bare hands. I'm getting out of here before they decide to come back for more."

They settled back into their hiding spot behind the clump of banana trees. "I've got one more idea," said Josh.

"What's that?" asked Ellen.

"I think we should sneak into Onamee's room at the top of the temple. We might find a clue, you know, something that might help us save Luna. We can't abandon her."

"But we can't just walk up the stairs. Remember what happened last time I almost broke the ancient tradition?"

"Yeah, that wasn't so good."

"Can I say something?" asked Will.

"Of course," replied Ellen.

"That's the dumbest idea I've ever heard."

She swatted him on the arm. "Be nice."

"This isn't the time to be nice. This is the time to be real. There is no way I'm going up there, and you guys shouldn't either. If you get caught, they'll kill you on the spot."

"Then why didn't they kill Ellen when she tried to step on the stairs?" asked Josh.

"I don't know. She's was lucky, I guess."

"It wasn't luck, it was God. He protected me," said Ellen.

"All right, so it was God. I agree with you. The point is, it's the Shaman's sacred territory up there. It's not the kind of place you mess around with. Why on earth would you want to risk going any-where near there?" asked Will.

"It's no big deal. All we have to do is go in, look around, and come back out. It won't take long, and maybe it will help. We won't know if we don't try," said Josh.

"But you've seen Onamee. You know how evil he is. Why take the chance?"

"I know it's dangerous. Do you think I'm stupid or something?" Josh grinned. "Wait, don't answer that. Really, I think this is our last chance. There's nothing else we can do. We've tried everything."

"I don't know, Josh. I have a funny feeling about this; and

besides, I still don't understand how we're supposed to get up there," said Ellen.

"What about the side window? I saw some vines growing up the side of the temple. They looked strong, and there's a tree nearby for backup. If the vines in the jungle can hold me and Puma, I'm sure these can hold me and Will."

"You and me? I don't think so." Will looked him square in the eye. "You're serious, aren't you?"

"This is our last chance. How many more times do I have to tell you that? I don't want to let Luna down; and to be totally honest, I'm kind of curious about what's up there," said Josh.

"What about me? What am I supposed to do?" asked Ellen. "I'm not going up, but you can't leave me behind. What if you get caught? Then I'm on my own."

"You can be the lookout. If you see anyone coming, signal us, and we'll come out," suggested Josh.

"Okay, as long as I don't have to go in."

Josh looked at his brother. "Are you coming?"

"Do I have any choice? I don't want you to go alone. Let's get this over with before I chicken out."

Ellen tugged on the thick vine dangling down the side of the temple. "It seems strong enough. You know, it's not too late. You guys can still back out. Are you sure you want to do this?"

"Absolutely sure," said Josh.

"Okay, then get going," ordered Will.

"Me? I'm not going first. You are. You know, oldest to youngest."

"I'm only a few minutes older than you. Besides, it's not my fault I was born first."

"It's not my fault either."

"I think the person who had the idea should go first. Josh, get moving," said Ellen.

"Yes, ma'am." He gave her a salute.

Josh climbed up the vine to the top of the tree and crawled across the branch nearest the window. He carefully eased one leg off the branch, swung it over the window ledge, and pulled his body through the opening. A second later, he poked his head out the window and waved to Ellen. She backed up to a spot where she could see the side window and the front staircase at the same time.

Will quickly followed Josh up. He poked his head out the window, and Ellen gave him the thumbs-up signal.

"I sure hope the Shaman's not here, because if he is, we'll be in big trouble," muttered Will.

It was dark inside the upper chamber because the tree leaves blocked most of the light. The air was cool and damp—unlike the hot, steamy jungle—and a faint sweet smell hung in the air. Bunches of dried plants were nailed to the beams that supported the ceiling, and baskets had been carefully arranged along the walls, holding dry, leathery animal skins and other shriveled things Josh couldn't recognize. The most remarkable thing in the room was an enormous wooden table. It had been placed exactly in the center of the room, and its sides and legs were covered with elaborate carvings, similar to the skulls on the side of the temple stairs.

"Is it my imagination, or does it feel kind of creepy in here?" whispered Josh.

"I feel like my skin's crawling with bugs or something. Hurry up. Let's get out of here."

The walls of the room were covered with pictures of terrible, violent scenes, painted in vivid colors. "Look, there's someone getting his head cut off," said Josh.

"That's disgusting. There's a picture of the cenote. That tied-up person must be a priestess. I don't like these drawings at all."

"Then don't look in the corner behind you, because there's a blow gun propped up beside a pile of shrunken heads."

Will turned around. "Yuck. I wish I hadn't looked. That's disgusting. Let's look at something else."

Josh walked over to the wooden table. A deep groove had been cut along the edge of the thick, wooden top, which acted like a trough.

Josh dipped his finger in. It came out coated in a dark brown liquid. "I think it's blood."

"Quit touching everything! You're going to get us into trouble."

"Okay. Sorry." He turned his attention back to the tabletop. Some little clay containers filled with dried powders were bunched in one corner, and a necklace of long, sharp teeth had been carefully arranged in the middle. "This must be another one of their idols," he said, pointing to a strange-looking carving.

"It looks like a snake," said Will.

"Maybe its Cha." Josh picked it up to take a closer look.

"Put that down! You said you wouldn't touch anything. Do you want the Shaman to know we were here?"

Josh didn't respond.

"Quit being such a pain," said Will.

Josh stood there, holding the carving, with a glazed look in his eyes.

"Are you okay?"

He didn't move.

"Come on, snap out of it. Okay, that's it. We're getting out of here."

Will ran over to the window. Ellen spotted him and gave him

the thumbs-up signal. He pointed to the rope so she would know they were coming down, and then he ran back to Josh, grabbed his wrists, and carefully moved his hands over the tabletop. He pried Josh's fingers off the carving one at a time, being careful not to touch it himself, until it clattered onto the table, spilling several containers of powder in the process.

The second Josh let go of the idol, he snapped out of his trance. "Where am I? What's going on?" he said.

"What do you mean, 'Where am I?' We're in the Shaman's lair at the top of the temple. Remember?"

"I don't think so."

"Are you okay?"

"I feel kind of dizzy. I need to get out of here."

"But look at the mess you made." Will pointed to the powder.

"I don't care. I need to get out of here."

Will ran back over to the window. Ellen was madly jumping up and down, waving her arms. "You're right. Someone's coming. Let's clean this up and get out."

The sound of footsteps drifted into the room. Whoever was coming was not far away.

"What should we do?" cried Josh.

"I don't know," said Will, looking at the mess. The footsteps were getting closer and closer.

"We have to go, now, before it's too late!"

The footsteps were just outside the doorway.

"Okay," said Will. He and Josh dashed across the room and jumped out the window.

The Shaman entered the room and immediately walked over to the table.

Josh and Will climbed across the tree branch and hid among the leaves.

The Shaman tapped his cane on the floor as he stared at the mess. "Someone has been in here." He walked over to the window.

A little monkey swung by.

"Oh, it was you again. Get lost, you furry little beast."

Josh and Will waited breathlessly in the tree for several long, long minutes.

"Do you think it's safe to go now? These branches are hurting my legs. I need to get down," whispered Will.

"But what about the Shaman? What if he sees us?" asked Josh.

"I think the coast is clear. Let's go."

The boys practically slid down the tree trunk. Josh let go when he was about one meter from the bottom. He landed on his feet, but then, still unsteady from his mission, he fell to the ground. "Ouch! That hurt!" he exclaimed.

Will carefully climbed down after him.

Ellen left her hiding place and helped Josh up. "Do you two know how close you came to getting caught?"

"I didn't know what to do. Something strange happened to Josh, and when I tried to help him, he spilled some of the Shaman's stuff. That slowed us down," said Will.

"What happened?"

"It felt like I was inside a nightmare," said Josh.

Ellen looked up at the top of the temple. There was no sign of the Shaman. "Let's get out of here before he finds us. It'll be safer to talk somewhere else."

The courtyard they had passed earlier was deserted, so they sat down on the log overlooking the ocean. "Josh, what happened in there? You seem really upset," observed Ellen.

"I don't know if I can talk about it. It was so horrible. I just want to forget it ever happened."

"What was so horrible?"

"I don't know, everything. The minute I touched that carving, bad feelings started flowing through my body, and then weird pictures came into my head, kind of like those paintings on the wall."

"What paintings on the wall?"

"There were pictures of people getting their heads cut off, and in one corner there was a pile of shrunken heads and a blowgun," said Will.

"Where did Josh find the carving?"

"On the wooden table in the middle of the room. There were a bunch of weird statues on it, like the one of the snake that Josh picked up, and little bottles of powder and other stuff. They spilled when he dropped it."

Josh shuddered. "It was so weird. While the pictures were flashing through my mind, I could hear people screaming and moaning, but I couldn't escape. It was like having a bad dream, except it was extra scary because I couldn't wake up and turn on the light."

"I knew I shouldn't have let you guys go up there. You could have been killed. I was sure you were going to get caught when I saw Onamee go up the steps."

"The main thing is that we're okay. God protected us," said Josh.

"If you weren't so stupid you wouldn't need so much protecting. Why do you always have to touch everything?" complained Will.

Ellen leaned over and put her arm around Josh. "It's over. Leave him alone. He learned his lesson."

"But you know I'm right."

"Give it up," ordered Ellen.

"Okay. We all need to give up this stupid rescue idea; and it's a good thing, because that was the last one of our plans."

Ellen sighed. "What a relief."

"Plans.... Hmm. That reminds me of something. Think, think, think," said Josh, pressing his fingers into his forehead. "Oh, I know: it's the verse we've been memorizing with Dad. '"I know the plans I have for you," declares the Lord. "Plans to prosper you and not to harm you, plans to give you hope and a future."'"

Will joined in, and they continued on together. "'"Then you will call upon me and come and pray to me, and I will listen to you. You will seek me and find me when you seek me with all your heart."'"

"It's from the book of Jeremiah," stated Will.

They sat there, staring out at the ocean, when suddenly a big smile flashed across Ellen's face. "That's it! You two are brilliant. You are so smart that I just have to hug you!" She leaned over and gave Will a big bear hug.

"Oh, no you don't!" said Josh, as she moved towards him. "I don't need any hugging."

Ellen put him in a headlock. "I love you, Joshua Donald MacKenzie. You got it. I can't believe I didn't think of it in the first place. How could I be so dumb?"

Josh wriggled out of her grasp. "Ellen, you're not making sense."

"Does she ever?" asked Will.

"Not very often. What are you talking about?"

Ellen was so happy, she didn't seem to even notice their insults. "It's the Bible verse—that's the answer. That's the plan! Come on, say it again, and this time think about what you're saying."

"We already said it. How's a Bible verse going to help us out here in the jungle?" asked Will.

"Just say the verse."

"Yes, boss," he growled.

"'"For I know the plans I have for you," declares the Lord, "plans to prosper you and not to harm you, plans to give you hope and a future."'" They continued on more boldly. "'"Then you will call upon me and come and pray to me, and I will listen to you. You will seek me and find me when you seek me with all your heart."'"

"We need to pray!" shouted Will. He punched his fist into the air. "Oh, sorry about that." He quickly pulled his arm back down to his side.

Josh gave him a funny look. "What's gotten into you? You never get that excited."

"I didn't mean to. It's just that I realized what the verse really means. We've been doing it all wrong. We tried to solve the problem ourselves instead of letting God take care of it. No wonder things aren't working out."

Ellen smiled. "Remember our cousin Abbie? She kept getting sicker and sicker, and everyone was worrying like crazy. After we finally had that family prayer meeting she started getting better."

"And remember when Dad lost his job? He and Mom were so worried. We all prayed, and he got a new job right away," said Will.

"And remember how relieved Mom was that he wouldn't have to travel so much? His new job was even better than the old one."

"Remember when we were really little and Mom was working and forgot to pick us up from school?" Will smiled. "Josh and I stood by the monkey bars and prayed that God would send someone to help us. Two minutes later, Uncle Andy drove by in his red truck. He took us home and stayed with us until Mom got back."

"We've had lots of answers to prayer, and I know if we pray right now and ask God to look after Luna instead of trying to do everything by ourselves, everything will work out," said Ellen. "I just know it."

As the sun set over the water, marking the end of another day, Josh, Will, and Ellen got down on their knees, bowed their heads, and talked to God.

"God, please be with Luna. We don't want the Shaman to wreck her life and hurt her family. Protect her from evil. You know we tried to rescue her. Maybe you can help her escape," prayed Will.

"And be with Puma, too. We know he needs you just as much as we do. Please help him understand so he can become a Christian, too," added Josh.

"God, please keep us safe. It's pretty dangerous here. Be with Mom and Dad, and help them not to miss us too much. We really miss them." Ellen sniffled. "And please help us get back home. Amen."

"Do you think we'll ever get back home?" asked Josh.

Ellen blinked back her tears. "I don't know. Only God knows."

TWELVE

The Ceremony

A thick and dreadful darkness fell over the village, and the ominous sound of drumming drifted through the night air, signaling the beginning of the Ascension of the Sun ceremony. Small bonfires had been lit beside the temple stairs, and a large fire burned in the center of the courtyard below. The men of the village guarded the entrance to the temple. Their bodies were striped with colorful paints, and bows and quivers of arrows hung down their backs. Many of the warriors wore plumes of feathers across their foreheads, and several of them had animal skins draped over their shoulders or tied around their waists. The women huddled in clusters farther back, their arms wrapped tightly around their children.

Josh, Will, and Ellen remained hidden in a clump of bushes off to one side of the courtyard. From their vantage point, they could easily watch the activity without being seen. Flaming torches made of bundled twigs were placed at the entrance of the path leading out to the cenote.

"Are you scared?" asked Josh.

"Why do you ask?" Ellen asked back.

"Because I am."

"I can feel the evil around us. It almost makes it hard to breathe.

If we stay behind these bushes, I think we'll be safe."

The drumming abruptly stopped, and the villagers turned and faced the temple.

"Look, there he is. He's standing in the doorway," whispered Will.

The Shaman emerged from the upper altar room, clothed in black from head to toe. Even his face was painted completely black. The only thing visible was his eyes. He turned to his right and then to his left, his head held high, like a king surveying his kingdom, and then slowly descended the stairs. The drumming started up again and grew faster and louder with each step. When he reached the bottom, he paused, lifted his arms up in front of him, and clapped his hands together. The drumming abruptly stopped.

"My people," he said in a deep, raspy voice, "we are here tonight at the temple of our fathers to pay homage to Cha."

The people responded by chanting: "Cha! Cha! Cha!"

"Who is the strongest of the gods?"

"Cha! Cha! Cha!"

"Who is the mightiest of the gods?" he shouted, lifting his arms into the air.

"Cha! Cha! Cha!"

"My people, Cha is the strongest and mightiest of the gods!"

The villagers whooped and clapped and stamped their feet.

"Our Cha is a mighty god and warrior, and he welcomes our new priestess tonight." He paused for a moment, and then with an evil gleam in his eye, he roared, "Let the ceremony begin."

The drummers slowly beat upon their drums as the Shaman walked back up the staircase. He reached his hand into the sack that hung across his chest. In one smooth motion, he grabbed a handful of powder and threw it in the air. A cloud of smoke enveloped him.

A moment later, when the smoke had cleared, the sound of many small gasps could be heard. A jaguar sat on the temple steps where the Shaman had been standing only a minute before.

The drumming stopped, and the jaguar let out a fierce growl. The warriors moved into position with their weapons. Another cloud of smoke appeared, the drummers pounded on their drums three times, and the Shaman reappeared. He walked through the smoke, down to the villagers, not stopping until he reached the bonfire burning in the center of the courtyard.

The villagers formed a circle around him. The drummers increased their tempo, pounding their palms against their drum skins in a smooth, mesmerizing motion. The villagers began to gently sway back and forth in time to the beat, and when the tempo increased, a group of them started to skip in a circle around the Shaman.

A group of dancers broke away from the circle and twirled around and around in the opposite direction. Beads of sweat coated their faces as they moved closer to the fire. They were one step away from the flames when the drummers pounded on their drums three more times, and everything stopped.

The Shaman shook his stick in the air. "Cha has revealed to me that we have traitors in our midst."

"Oh, no! He sees us. We're doomed," groaned Will.

"Wait a minute. Maybe it's not us," murmured Ellen.

The villagers glanced anxiously at one another. A wave of whispers passed through the crowd.

The Shaman looked straight at the bushes where they were hiding. "There are three visitors in our midst who doubt me and the power of Cha."

"He sees us. Let's make a run for it!" whispered Will.

"I'm not running. Let's get this over with." Josh stood up and took a step forward. Will tried to grab his leg to stop him, but he missed and fell flat on his face.

"I'm one of your visitors," said Josh, "and I don't worship Cha. I worship God. He's the one with the real power."

Ellen crawled out of the bushes and stood up beside him. Will grabbed both of them by the legs. "What are you doing?" he hissed.

"Saying what's true," said Josh.

"Approach me, traitors," commanded the Shaman.

Ellen bent over and grabbed Will by the arm. "Come on, get up." He managed to stand up beside her.

Josh was so scared that his legs couldn't move. The villagers quickly lost patience and surrounded them. He grabbed Ellen's hand. "I think we're really in trouble," he whispered.

"What are we going to do? I … I … I think I'm going to …" Will keeled over, banging his head on the bony shoulder of one of the elderly villagers in front of him.

"Oh, no, not again," groaned Ellen. She and Josh grabbed Will under the arms and dragged him along as the crowd surged towards the Shaman.

"Children," he began quietly, "our village needs good weather—rain to make our crops grow, and sunlight on our fields so we can feed our people. Cha wants our village to prosper. How dare you try to take this away from us? Who is your God that he would do this?" he shouted, shaking his stick at them.

"Our God is a God of love. We don't need to take defenseless young girls like Luna away from their families and make them into priestesses so we can get rain. That's not how our God takes care of his people," insisted Ellen.

"So this is about Luna, just as I expected. Bring her!" he commanded.

The three guards brought Luna out from the hut at the side of the temple. Her wrists were bound together. She dragged her feet in the dirt, trying to hold the guards back, but it was no use. They lifted her up and carried her to the Shaman. She squirmed fiercely in their arms until they put her down in front of the temple steps.

"Here is your friend," said the Shaman. Luna tried to run away, but two guards stepped in front of her, blocking her path.

"She will bring our village rain, and there is nothing you can do to stop it." A low, rumbling laughter escaped from his throat. "Guards, untie her. Luna, say goodbye," he commanded.

"We have to do something. This isn't working," moaned Josh.

"But what?" asked Ellen.

"I don't know. Anything."

Ellen took a deep breath. "Mr. Shaman, why do you even bother with this ceremony? Last year you made another girl into a priestess, and Puma told us you still had a bad harvest. You have no guarantee this ceremony will even do anything."

"How dare you question Cha! Guards, bring Puma. He has spoken poorly of Cha, so he will join his sister at the cenote."

"No, don't take him! He hasn't done anything wrong," exclaimed Ellen.

"Oh, yes, child, he has. Those who doubt the power of Cha will suffer the consequences."

"Your Cha isn't a god. He's not even real. He's just a carving of a snake that you made yourself. Our God is real. He's the only one who can help you."

"Well, you'd better call on your God right now, because you're going to need all the help you can get. You and your brothers are about to go for a little swim." Josh cringed as the Shaman's laughter echoed through the village.

The Shaman reached into his bag and vanished behind another cloud of smoke. When it blew away, the jaguar was back on the steps, baring its teeth to the crowd. It crouched, ready to attack.

In the midst of all the excitement, Will had come to. "If the Shaman doesn't get us, that jaguar will. I don't want to die out here in the jungle," he moaned.

"Pray. That's all we can do now. Just pray," said Ellen. She bowed her head. "Jesus, I know you love us. We've tried to say and do the right things here tonight. We need you now. Please, please save us."

Another cloud of smoke appeared, and the Shaman returned. The drummers began playing again, but this time there seemed to be a greater urgency to their rhythm. The Shaman raised his stick into the air. "Make way for the priestess! She will serve Cha forever!" He led the procession of villagers through the village. The guards grabbed Josh, Will, Ellen, Puma, and Luna, and pulled them into the line.

"Please, God, please help us. Things are really bad. We need you," whispered Josh.

When they reached the edge of the jungle, the Shaman turned and faced the kids. "So tell me, children, where is your God now?"

THIRTEEN

The Storm

A strong wind rolled off the ocean and blew its way through the crowd of villagers, whipping their hair into their faces and extinguishing the bonfires at the base of the temple. Thick smoke filled the air. A flock of seagulls screamed overhead, followed by a dark cloud, which settled over the village.

A hush fell over the villagers. No one moved. A clap of thunder sounded and echoed off into the jungle. The ground began to tremble, and sharp bursts of lightning filled the night sky.

Josh's head started to pound, and his stomach churned. He closed his eyes. "God, I know you're here. The Bible says you're always with us. Please help us."

The villagers looked to the Shaman, unsure of what to do; but he stood firm, his fists clenched above his head. The wind grew stronger. It smashed against the stone buildings and tore the straw roofs off the huts. Bolt after bolt of lightning arced across the sky, filling it with a beautiful yet terrifying display of light.

The cloud above the village gathered over the temple. Josh saw a look of fear flash across the Shaman's face. Lightning burst from the cloud and struck the very top stone. Its sheer power split the stone in two, and the heavy blocks tumbled to the ground.

In the roar of the wind, Josh could hear a still, small voice. It seemed to be saying, "God Almighty … King of Glory … I Am Who I Am."

Sheets of rain came pouring out of the sky, and the frightened villagers scattered in every direction; but no matter where they ran, they could not escape the forces of nature being unleashed around them. No one could hide from Josh, Will, and Ellen's God.

In all the commotion, the guards let go of their prisoners. Puma untied his sister, and she ran towards the edge of the village.

"Don't let her get away. We've got to catch her before she vanishes into the jungle!" shouted Josh. He and Will sprinted after her.

Onamee grabbed the back of Ellen's dress, and pulled her towards him. He wrapped his arm around her neck and squeezed until he could hear her gasping for air.

"Well, young girl, we'll see who's the strongest and the mightiest now."

The boys had run a little ways into the jungle when Will stopped to catch his breath. "Where's Ellen?"

"I thought she was right behind us," said Josh.

"We must have lost her."

"We better go back and find her."

They raced back to the village. The storm had ended as abruptly as it had come, but the rain had turned the village grounds into a slippery mess. One of the worker's huts had been struck by lightning, and now the entire area was engulfed in flames. As they ran through the village, there was not a person or animal in sight. The mud on the path was ankle deep in places, and palm branches littered the ground.

"What's going on? A few minutes ago this was one of the most beautiful places on earth, but look at it now," observed Will.

"Where did everyone go? They couldn't have left already."

"I think they've abandoned the village. How are we ever going to find Ellen in this mess?" Without the leafy canopy of the jungle to protect them, the boys were soaking wet and covered in mud from head to toe. "I don't want to stand here waiting forever," said Will.

"I don't see Ellen anywhere. Do you think she went into the jungle on a different path?"

"I don't know. How long should we keep looking for her?"

As they rounded the corner by the temple, the boys stopped dead in their tracks. The huge stones from the temple were scattered everywhere, some of them lying upside down and others turned on their sides, like a pile of toy blocks that had been knocked over. Not one was left standing on top of another. Despite the fact that the temple was demolished, the wooden altar from the upper room stood untouched in the midst of the ruins. Ellen lay on top of it, motionless.

Josh ran over to her. "Ellen, Ellen," he said, gently slapping her cheeks. She opened her left eye a crack and twitched her head to that side. "Come on, Ellen, wake up." He looked over to Will. "We've got to get her out of here. Help me untie her."

Will looked down at her hands and feet. "There's nothing to untie. She's just lying here."

"What do you mean?"

"She's not tied up. I don't know why she's not moving. It's like she's frozen." He wrung his hands together as he stared at his sister.

"Come on, Ellen, wake up. Please? You can do it. We've gone

this far. Don't blow it now." Josh lifted her head and shoulders up, but she was as limp as a rag doll, and she fell back onto the table.

"Your sister won't be waking up," rang out a deep voice. Onamee stepped out from behind one of the fallen stones. His robe was in shreds, and all that was left of his war paint was a few uneven streaks, but he still carried his walking stick. "Luna may have escaped, but your sister will not."

"You can't have her. She's our sister. We need her," shouted Josh.

The Shaman shoved him to the ground. Will was so angry that he took a run at him, hoping to bowl him over, but he completely missed the Shaman and ended up skidding out in the mud behind him.

"Give up, boys. It's too late for her," warned the Shaman.

"What do you mean, 'too late'? What have you done to her?" said Josh.

"There are many ways to please Cha. Choosing a priestess is only one of them. I gave your sister a special potion prepared from the venom of the rattlesnake. It will cause her to fall into a deep sleep before it stops her breathing. Your sister will feel no pain as she leaves this world for the darkness of the next. Her death will appease Cha and allow him to restore my village," he said, sweeping his arm to take in all the ruins, "the village that you and your God have destroyed."

"No! Keep her out of it," shouted Josh. He lashed out at the Shaman. His fist connected with Onamee's nose, and large drops of crimson blood dripped onto the Shaman's lips and chin. Onamee stood there, cradling his nose in his hand, his eyes burning with hatred.

"Stop whatever you're doing to my sister. You can undo it. Fix it right now, or I'll do that again," threatened Josh.

"Only I have the antidote, and you're not going t[...]
Besides, it's time for you to join your sister." The Sha[...]
a large dagger from beneath his robe and held it in f[...]
he moved towards Josh.

Josh backed up several steps until his heel connected with one
of the stones from the temple. "Oh no, I'm trapped," he groaned.

The Shaman closed in on him, slicing the air between them
with his dagger. "Your time in Quinaroo is finished," he growled.

Just then, out of the corner of his eye, Josh saw Puma creep up
behind the Shaman. In one smooth burst of movement, Puma
jumped onto the Shaman's back and grabbed the hand holding the
dagger. It flew through the air and landed in a pile of rubble out of
reach. The two of them fell to the ground and rolled back and forth
on top of each other. It was a close match. The Shaman was bigger,
but Puma was faster and stronger.

Josh and Will ran over and grabbed the Shaman's arms until
Puma accidentally kicked Will. "Ouch," he cried. He grabbed his leg
as he jumped up and down.

"Get out of the way. I've got to stop him. We need your God.
He's the one with the true power," panted Puma.

The Shaman rolled on top of him, pinning him to the ground by
the shoulders. In one final burst of energy, Puma jerked his legs up
and slammed his feet into the back of the Shaman's skull. The
maneuver took Onamee by surprise, and he fell forwards. Josh heard
a crack as his head hit one of the stones.

He fell on his side and lay there motionless, except for his eye-
lids, which twitched open and closed. Blood poured from his ears,
pooling on the ground beneath him. Puma crawled over to him, but
before he could do anything, the Shaman gasped, his entire body
shuddered, and he stopped breathing.

The boys stood there, shell-shocked. "I think he's dead," mum-
led Josh. "I've never seen a dead person before."

Puma put his ear against the Shaman's chest. "You're right. He's
not a threat to us anymore."

"But what about Ellen?" asked Will.

Puma jumped to his feet and ran over to the altar where Ellen
lay. "What did he do to her?"

"He said something about giving her poison from a rattlesnake."

"Oh, no," groaned Puma. "We don't have long. It might already
be too late."

"Too late? What do you mean, 'too late'?" stammered Josh.

"Rattlesnake venom acts quickly. It stops the victim's breathing."

"The Shaman said he had the antidote. Where does he keep it?"
asked Will.

"How would I know?"

Will's eyes filled with tears. "This is your village. You're supposed
to know these things. Ellen needs it."

"I don't know where it is."

"Stop arguing and go look for it. You're wasting valuable time,"
ordered Josh.

"Ellen's going to die. How will we ever live without her?" said
Will. He fell to the ground, sobbing.

"Do you really think you'll miss me?" she whispered.

"What?" Will looked up at his sister.

She opened one eye. "I asked if you'll miss me?"

"Ellen, you're okay. Look everyone, Ellen's okay!" Will gave her
a big hug.

Puma scratched his head. "What's going on? You're supposed to
be dying."

Ellen sat up. "The Shaman gave me a strange concoction to drink, but I spit it out when he wasn't looking."

"So you were just pretending to be unconscious?" asked Josh.

"I knew there was no point in fighting, so I thought I'd wait and try to escape."

"As soon as you saw he was dead you could have told me you were okay. I can't believe you let me make a fool out of myself," complained Will.

"I tried to tell you before. Didn't you see me open my eye a crack and shake my head towards the Shaman? He was behind you. I thought you'd figure it out. At least now I know who loves me and would really miss me."

Will smiled.

"I'd miss you a little bit," said Josh, with just a hint of a grin on his face.

"I know you would. Help me down. We need to go find Luna."

"We'd better hurry. It's not safe in the jungle at night. She could be in just as much danger out there as she was in here," said Puma.

"Great. Just what we need, more danger," muttered Will.

"Let's go before it's too late," said Ellen.

"Stop," panted Will. "I need air. I can't breath!"

Ellen kept running. "We can't stop now. We've got to find Luna. I need to know if she's okay."

"How on earth do you expect to find her in the middle of the jungle? It will be impossible. This jungle's huge, and I can't see a thing. We need a searchlight or something," said Josh.

"I don't know how we're going to find her," and then with a fierce determination that surprised Josh, she added, "but I'm not leaving here until we do."

"I guess you're right. It would be terrible, if after all this, we lost her out here in the jungle."

"But what if we get hurt finding her?" griped Will.

"Relax. Everything will be okay. All we have to do is tell her that the temple was destroyed and Onamee is dead. She's safe now. After we find her, we can take her home to her mom," said Ellen.

"I hope their house is still okay," added Josh.

They ran a little farther. "I feel like I've been here before, you know, like déjà vu. It seems familiar, somehow," commented Ellen.

Josh and Will looked at her, and in a split second, all three of them understood. "We're in the picture on the wall, aren't we?" said Josh.

"Let's go!" shouted Ellen. They surged down the path with more energy than ever before.

A minute later, they found themselves in a small clearing. The rain had slowed to a drizzle, and a bit of moonlight had managed to find its way through the treetops. Josh could barely see Luna's silhouette. She sat on a fallen log in the middle of the clearing, with Aqua resting contentedly on her wrist.

Puma ran up and hugged her. "Are you okay?"

Luna burst into tears. "Oh, Puma, I was so scared," she sobbed.

"Aawk. So scared. So scared," said Aqua.

"Oh, Aqua, be quiet." Luna gently stroked her bird's feathered head. "I thought I was going to die. Our friends saved me. I'm so glad I don't have to be a priestess."

"We didn't do anything. God did all the work," said Ellen.

"Aawk. God did. God did."

Puma let go of his sister and walked over to Ellen. "I was wrong to doubt you and your God. You're right, your God saved us. Cha is nothing. Your God is everything. It's hard for me to say this, but the truth is that my village has been following the wrong god for a long time. What should I do?"

"You need to pray. You need to ask Jesus into your heart and promise to follow him. Can you do that?" she asked.

"After what I've seen today, I know I don't have a choice. Can I do it right now?"

"Of course," said Ellen. The two of them bowed their heads. "Dear God, thank you so much for showing Puma and all the people in his village that you are the one true God," she prayed.

"That's right. You are the only true God, and I need to follow you," added Puma

"And, God, please forgive them for following Cha and believing in the Shaman's evil ways."

"Yes, I'm sorry we followed the wrong god. I want to do things right."

Ellen opened her eyes. "Now you need to ask Jesus into your heart. I can't do that part for you."

"But I don't know how to do that. How is he supposed to go inside my body, into my heart?"

"It's more like he goes into your soul, you know, the part of you that lives on after you die. He won't put his physical body into yours. It's more like his Spirit joins with your spirit and lives with you."

"I'm not sure I understand."

"Just ask him to come. Tell him you want to follow him and learn to be more like him. Does that make sense?"

"Sort of." Puma took a deep breath. "Jesus, Ellen tells me that you love me. I believe her. Please come live with me right now so I can be one of your people, too. I'll try my very best to live the way you want me to."

"Amen," said Ellen.

"Aawk. Amen. Amen."

Everyone burst out laughing. "I guess Aqua likes to pray, too," said Luna.

"Why do you say 'amen'?" asked Puma.

"It's the way we end our prayers. It means we're leaving things with God, and we'll wait for him to work them out."

"I think I have a lot to learn."

"Actually, we all have a lot to learn. God doesn't expect us to know everything all at once. The main thing is that we keep learning and trusting in him. I know it's dumb, but so often we try to do things ourselves instead of waiting for God to lead the way. What happened today was a perfect example—we wanted to rescue Luna, but failed miserably, and instead God saved her and your whole village in one awesome display of his power. I'm still having a hard time believing that a lightning bolt destroyed the temple."

Luna gave Ellen a shy glance. "Can I pray that prayer too?"

Ellen smiled. "Of course."

"Wait! Look! Your housecoat! It's lying on the ground over there," exclaimed Josh.

"This must be the clearing where we landed. I guess it fell off the tree." Ellen walked over and picked it up. Water poured out of it. She put her hand in the pocket and let out a shriek of joy as she pulled out Josh's stone.

"I don't believe it. This is fantastic! Maybe now we can go home," said Will.

"There's just one problem: we don't know how it works. How are we supposed to get home if we don't know what to do?" Josh rubbed his forehead. "Think, think, think."

"Why do you want to go home? You can't leave us now," said Puma.

"I need to pray with you first," said Luna.

"And if you go, who will take you swimming in the ocean? Who's going to teach you how to swing on jungle vines and how to eat caterpillars? Who will tell us about Jesus?"

Suddenly the jungle started spinning. Josh saw a dark tornado-like tunnel come rolling towards them.

"YES!" he yelled, with a big smile on his face. "We're going home!"

"No, don't go!" cried Puma.

"Bye!" yelled Josh.

"You'll be okay. Make sure you pray with Luna," said Ellen.

The tornado picked them up, and Puma and Luna were left standing alone in the dark, steamy jungle.

— FOURTEEN —

Back Home

When Josh woke up, he was back in his bedroom. Blankets, pillows, and dirty laundry were strewn all over the floor. He rubbed the grit out of his eyes and leaned over the side of his bed. Ellen and Will were just waking up on the bunk below.

"Guys, I just had the strangest dream. We were in a jungle somewhere. It was so weird."

"No way. I had a dream about a jungle too. In my dream I was swimming in the ocean with this jungle guy from a village called Quinaroo," said Will.

"You were what? That's amazing! I had the exact same dream too, except at the end there was this gigantic storm," exclaimed Ellen.

"Storm? Would that be a storm with a lightning bolt—" asked Will.

"—that split the temple in two?" finished Josh. An eerie silence filled the room. "How could we all have had the same dream?"

"Maybe it wasn't a dream. Maybe it really happened," suggested Will.

"No," they all said together, shaking their heads.

"Boys, are you in there?" Their mother opened the door. "Oh …

Ellen, you're here too. And it's so messy in here. This room absolutely has to be cleaned up today, and don't give me any excuses about how you don't have time. You don't have to live like pigs, you know."

"Mom, don't you want to tell me how much you missed me?" said Josh.

"I don't usually miss you while you're asleep. It's been only a few hours since I kissed you goodnight, silly." She reached over and tousled his hair. "You say the strangest things sometimes."

"You mean you saw me a few hours ago?"

"Yes, when I tucked you in. Why do you ask?"

"I don't know, it just seemed like we'd been apart longer."

"Whatever you say, dear. It's time to get up. You can't stay in bed all day, and besides, we've got lots to do. I made each of you a list of chores." They all groaned. "And before I forget, remember that we have a special church service tomorrow. A missionary from Central America is speaking. He's from a little place called Quinaroo, I think. You know how much your father loves to listen to missionaries. He won't want to miss a single word."

"Mom, where did you say the missionary was from?" asked Ellen.

"A little village called Quinaroo—I think that's how you pronounce it."

"Quinaroo. Hmm, it rhymes with poo," said Josh. His brother and sister started to giggle.

"Isn't it a little early in the day for toilet humor?" asked his mother.

"Yes, Mother," he said in his most serious voice. "I was thinking of Winnie the Pooh."

"Joshua Donald MacKenzie, that's enough," she scolded. "Apparently all the people in this village became Christians many years ago after a missionary family went to live with them."

"Missionaries went there to live with them?" exclaimed Ellen.

"You know, dear, it happens all the time." She tilted her head to one side and looked them over. "Something's different. Have you three been in some sort of trouble?"

A jolt of terror seized Josh's heart. "Like what?"

"I don't know. You just seem a little off this morning. Anyhow, the people that are speaking in church are the descendants of the original missionaries. They're even showing a video. They hold their church services in this magnificent old temple that overlooks the ocean. A friend of mine visited the place last year, and she said it was beautiful. They rebuilt the temple, took out all the idols, and put a cross inside. It sounds very interesting. Now, please get up. We have a busy day." She gently closed the door behind her.

"I don't believe it. This must be a coincidence," said Will.

Ellen stood up. "I don't know. Maybe this is how God works. He's been doing all kinds of things we'd never expected."

"There's just one thing I don't understand," said Josh.

"What's that?" asked Ellen.

"How did the Shaman do all that magic?"

"It's not that hard if you know what to do. You just have to practice a lot," advised Will.

"Practice?"

"Yeah. You have to practice, you know, like lighting the powder from his pouch so the smoke appears. It probably took him awhile to get that just right so he could fool the villagers."

"What are you talking about? He sure fooled me."

"I don't know exactly how he did it, but you can make smoke out of potassium nitrate and sugar."

"How do you know that? You're just making this up so we'll

think you're smart," teased Josh.

"You already know I'm smart. I learned how to do that from the chemistry set I got for Christmas last year."

"But where would he get potassium from?"

"You can make it from ashes and dirt. It would probably take a while to purify it, but it could be done."

"Oh, brother. How come you know everything?"

"I don't know quite everything yet." Will crossed his arms and smiled, looking quite pleased with himself.

Ellen sat back down. "What about the jaguar? That had to have been magic."

"Do you want me to explain that to you too?" asked Will.

"Okay."

"That whole jaguar thing was an optical illusion. Did you notice how the Shaman always vanished in a cloud of smoke right before the jaguar appeared?"

"I didn't think about it at the time, but you're right."

"He used the smoke to hide the jaguar while it was being moved into position."

"What about the poison he gave Ellen?" asked Josh.

"I know the answer to that one," she replied.

"Well, at least it's not my know-it-all brother for once," said Josh.

"Be nice. It's not Will's fault he's so smart." She and Will beamed at each other. "Don't you want to know the Shaman's secret?"

"Okay, tell me."

"A lot of the medicine we use today was discovered in the rain forest. The Shaman would have learned about the properties of different plants and animals from his father and grandfather. They pass that sort of knowledge down through their families."

"Thank you, smart girl. Now leave me alone, okay," grumbled Josh.

"Does that answer your questions, or do you want us to tell you more?" asked Will.

Josh groaned. "You guys are pathetic. I have to think about this for a while. I thought the Shaman was this super powerful guy, but it was all an act. It really bugs me that he tricked everyone. How am I supposed to know what to believe?"

He climbed down from the top bunk, and Will and Ellen burst out laughing.

"What?"

By now Ellen was laughing so hard she was crying. Will lay on the bed, rolling back and forth as he clutched his stomach.

A big smile crossed Josh's face. He struck a muscle pose and gave his best Tarzan imitation.

"If I wasn't wearing this," he said, pointing to his loincloth, "I'd never have believed any of this either."

The End.

Trust in the LORD with all your heart

and lean not on your own understanding;

in all your ways acknowledge him,

and he will make your paths straight.

Proverbs 3:5–6

Rescue in the Mayan Jungle

Life Issue: I want to put God first in my life.
Spiritual Building Block: Worship

Think About It

 Do the following activities to grow in your love for God:

Read the story of God giving the Ten Commandments to Moses (Exodus 19-20). Try to imagine what it would be like to be one of the people in the story. The people had to prepare before they could receive these important words. They washed their clothes, purified themselves, and set up boundary lines at the bottom of the mountain that no one except Moses and Aaron could cross—because if they saw God face to face, they would die.

Imagine how it would have felt if you had been there that day. Lightning flashed across the sky, a trumpet blasted, smoke filled the air, and God descended from heaven in a blazing fire. The people were probably terrified; they must have wanted to run and hide, or even just look away, but they couldn't. The beautiful, yet frightening, sight of God mesmerized them.

How do you usually think about God? Do you think of him as a buddy or Santa Claus? The story of the Ten Commandments gives us a picture of God as holy, powerful, and awesome—so different than we often imagine. We are to love him and fear him.

How do you usually think about the Ten Commandments? Do you think of them as a list of do's and don'ts? Actually, they are ten concepts that explain how we are to relate to God and others. They tell us what kind of people we should be and how to live a life that is pleasing to God. God gave us the Commandments because he loves us and wants us to understand what is important to him.

Talk About It

 Do the following activities to grow in your love for God:

Rescue in the Mayan Jungle is a story about the first Commandment: "You shall have no other gods before me." God revealed himself in a special way to Josh, Will, and Ellen, much like he did to the Israelites at Mount Sinai. The people of Quinaroo had been worshiping Cha, a carving of a snake. When Ellen and the boys tried to help Luna and boldly proclaimed the power of God to the villagers, their lives were in danger. God came to their rescue, saved them, and showed his mighty power to the villagers. As a result, everyone came to understand God's love and faithfulness in a new way.

Sit down with a parent or teacher or a pastor and talk about how much you love God and how much he loves you. Saying these things out loud will help you appreciate God more, and it will also encourage the person you are talking to.

If you don't feel as though you love God as much as you think you should—if you know that you love other stuff more—talk about that, too. Being open and honest will help you overcome difficult things. Ask the other person to pray with you so that God will help you put him first.

Ask the people who are close to you—parents, brothers, sisters, friends—if they can see that you love God. Have they noticed your life is different because of your love for him? If they see that in you, thank God. If not, ask them to help you figure out what can you do tomorrow to let God's love shine in your life. Ask God to help you find different ways to show others his love.

Try It

 Do the following activities to grow in your love for God:

Find a compass and go for a walk, trying to move only north. If an obstacle prevents you from going this direction, take a few steps west and then a few steps north and then the same number of steps east to get back on track.

Our minds are like the needle on a compass. Even though we may think about lots of different things throughout the day, we always go back to the things we love the most, just like the needle on a compass always points north.

Pay attention to the things you think about. What's the first thing you think about when you wake up, and what is your last thought before going to sleep? A favorite television show? Sports? Friends? Stuff? When you have extra money or spare time, how do you use it? Are you making the things of your life more important than God?

The Israelites saw God's mighty display of power on the mountaintop in a way that no people had ever seen before. You'd think that after witnessing something that amazing, they would have no trouble following him, but that's not what happened. They got tired of waiting for Moses to come back down the mountain, so they gathered up their gold jewelry and made an idol of a calf to worship (Exodus 32). Pray to God throughout each day so that you will stay focused on him. He knows we get sidetracked easily, just as the Israelites did. If we don't go through each day with our hearts pointed towards God, we'll start to love other things more than we love him. It's not always easy, but we need to follow God every day of our lives, not because we know it's the right thing to do, but because we love him.

Memorize a passage of scripture that will help you to put God first. Josh, Will, and Ellen memorized Jeremiah 29:11–12. "'For I know the plans I have for you,' declares the LORD, 'plans to prosper you and not to harm you, plans to give you hope and a future. Then you will call upon me and come and pray to me, and I will listen to you. You will seek me and find me when you seek me with all your heart.'"

One of the best parts about loving God is that even when we turn away, he will always take us back. If we call out to him and look for him, we will always find him. You can count on it!